Disney
ZOOTOPIA

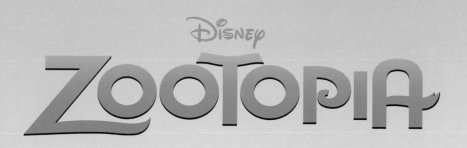

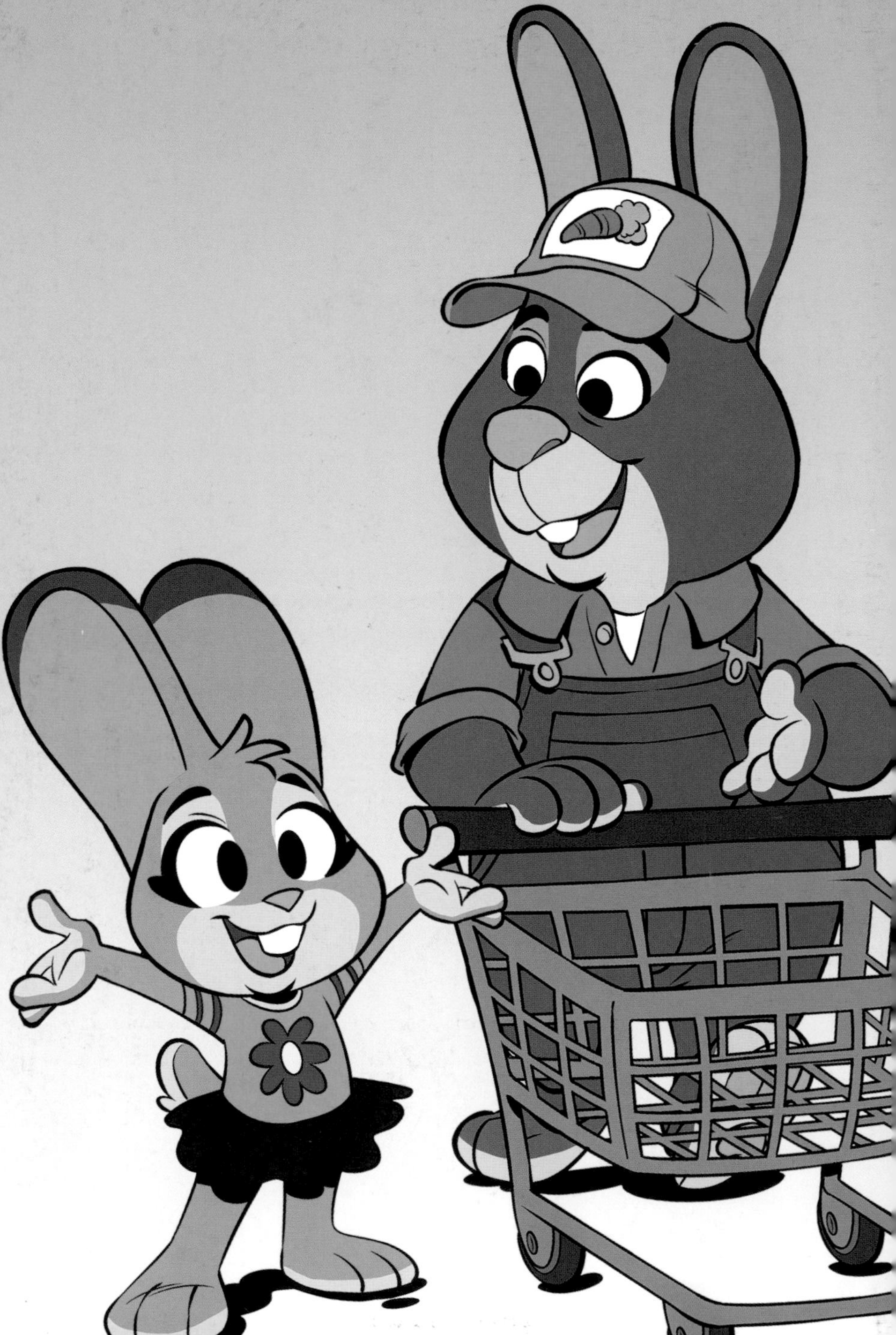

Disney ZOOTOPIA

FAMILY NIGHT

Script by
Jimmy Gownley

Art by
Leandro Ricardo da Silva

Colors by
Wes Dzioba

Lettering by
Chris Dickey

Dark Horse Books

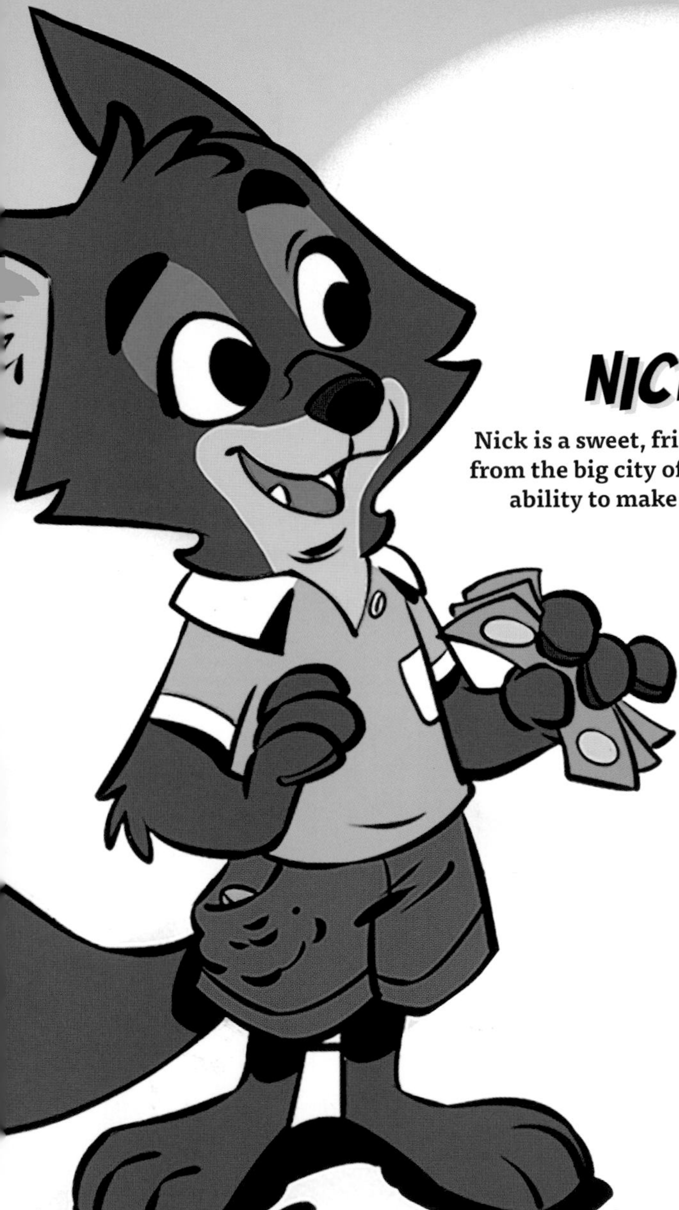

NICK WILDE

Nick is a sweet, friendly, and mischievous fox from the big city of Zootopia. He has a natural ability to make others smile and laugh.

JUDY HOPPS

Judy is an energetic, clever, and big-hearted bunny from the rural town of Bunnyburrow. She loves helping others and will lend a paw at any chance she gets.

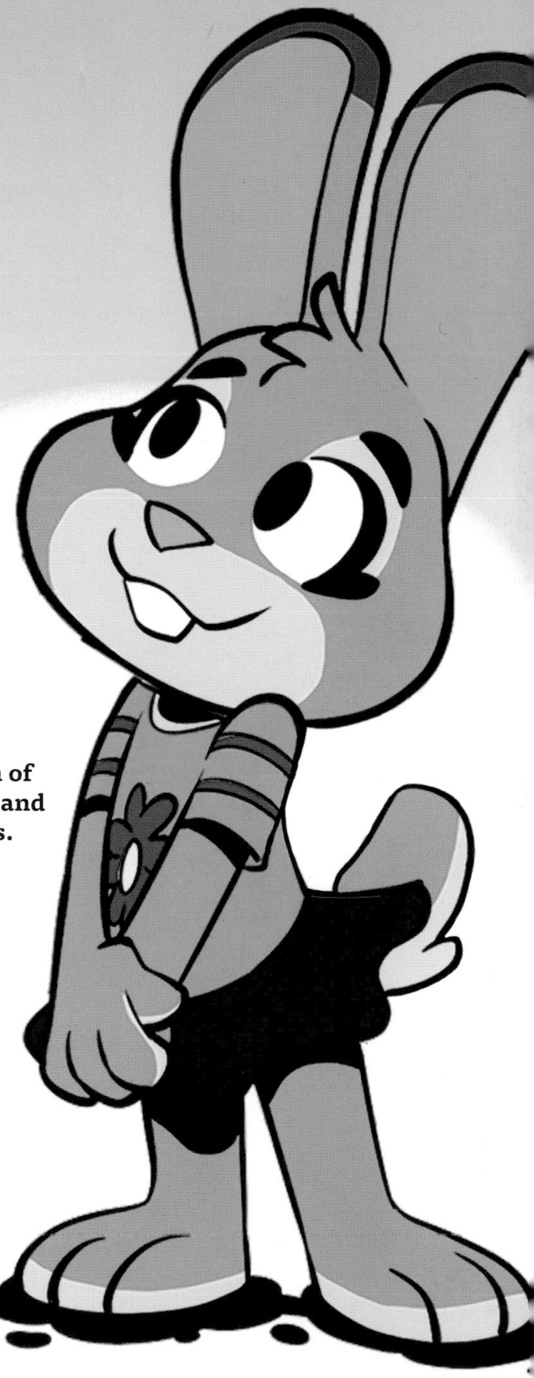

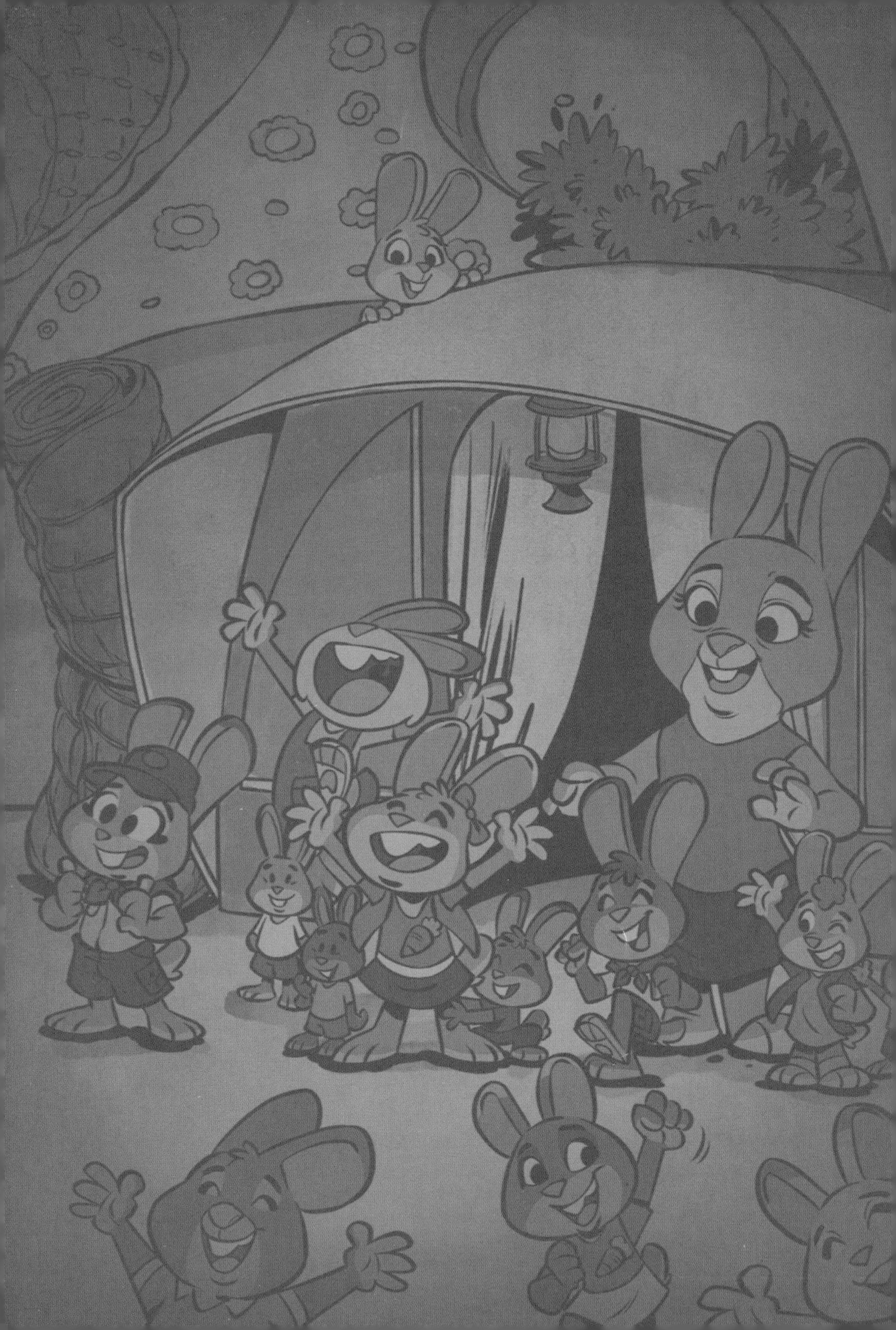

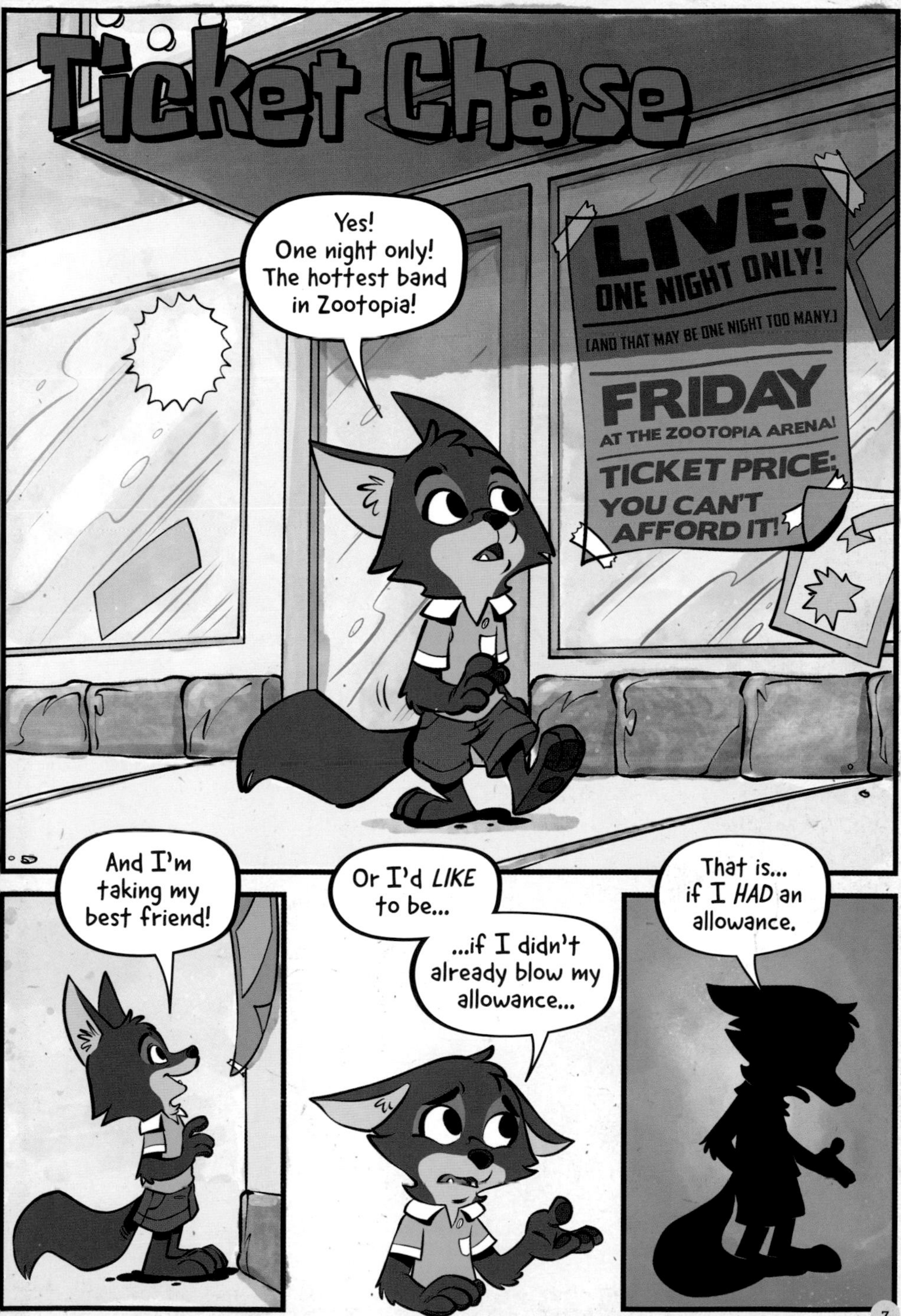
Ticket Chase
Yes! One night only! The hottest band in Zootopia!
LIVE! ONE NIGHT ONLY!
[AND THAT MAY BE ONE NIGHT TOO MANY.]
FRIDAY AT THE ZOOTOPIA ARENA!
TICKET PRICE: YOU CAN'T AFFORD IT!
And I'm taking my best friend!
Or I'd *LIKE* to be...
...if I didn't already blow my allowance...
That is... if I *HAD* an allowance.

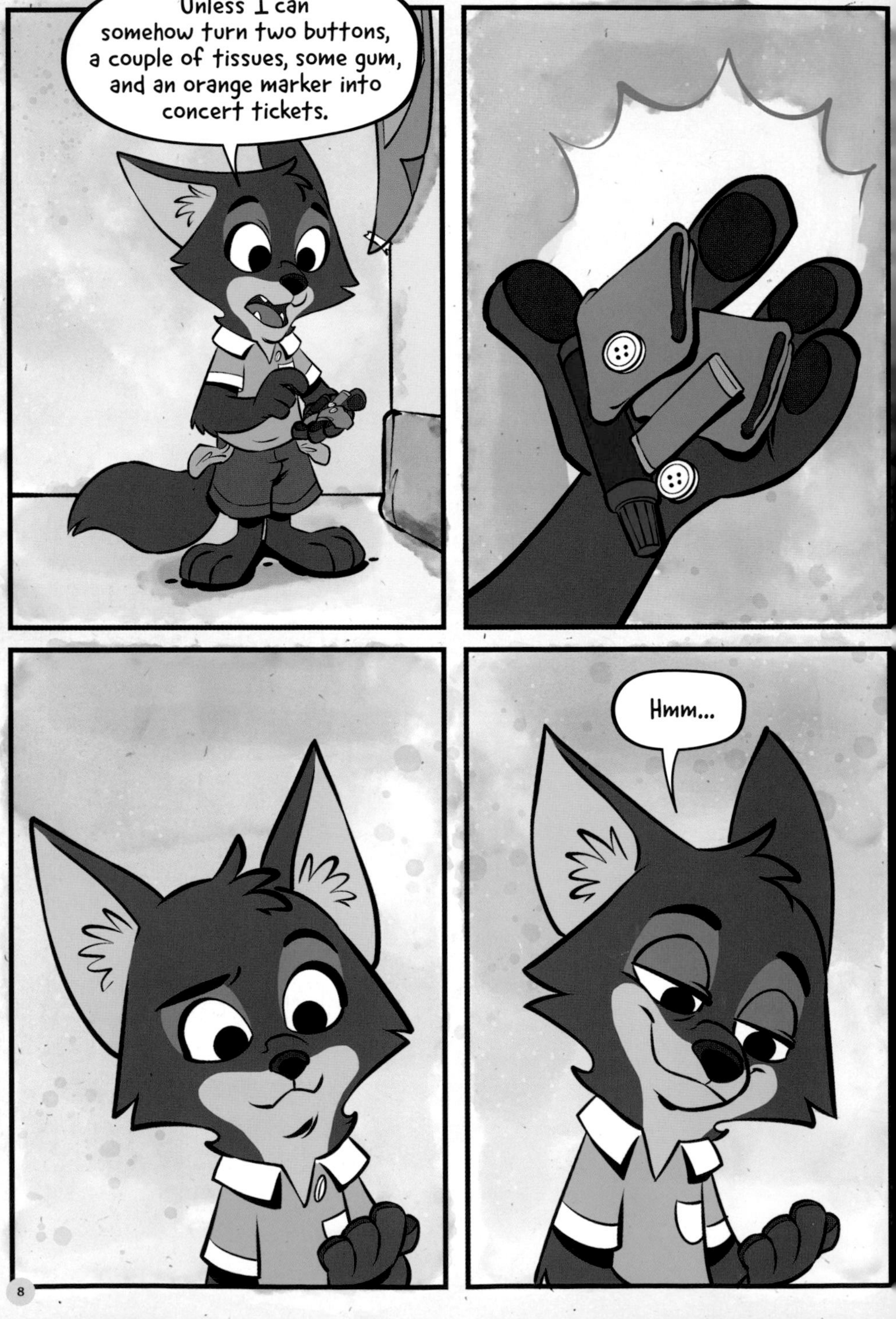
Unless I can somehow turn two buttons, a couple of tissues, some gum, and an orange marker into concert tickets.
Hmm...

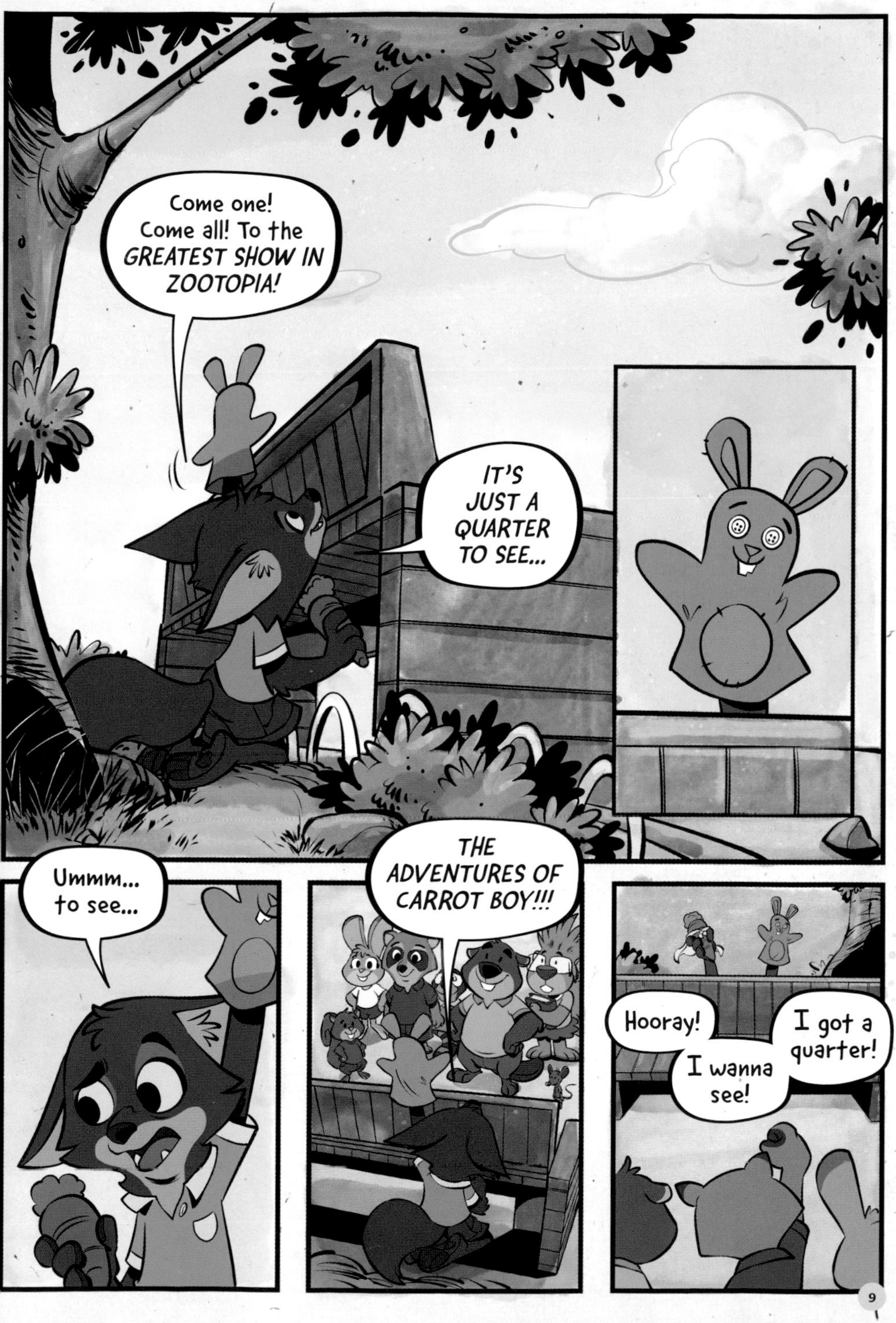
Come one!
Come all! To the *GREATEST SHOW IN ZOOTOPIA!*
IT'S JUST A QUARTER TO SEE...
Ummm... to see...
THE ADVENTURES OF CARROT BOY!!!
Hooray!
I wanna see!
I got a quarter!

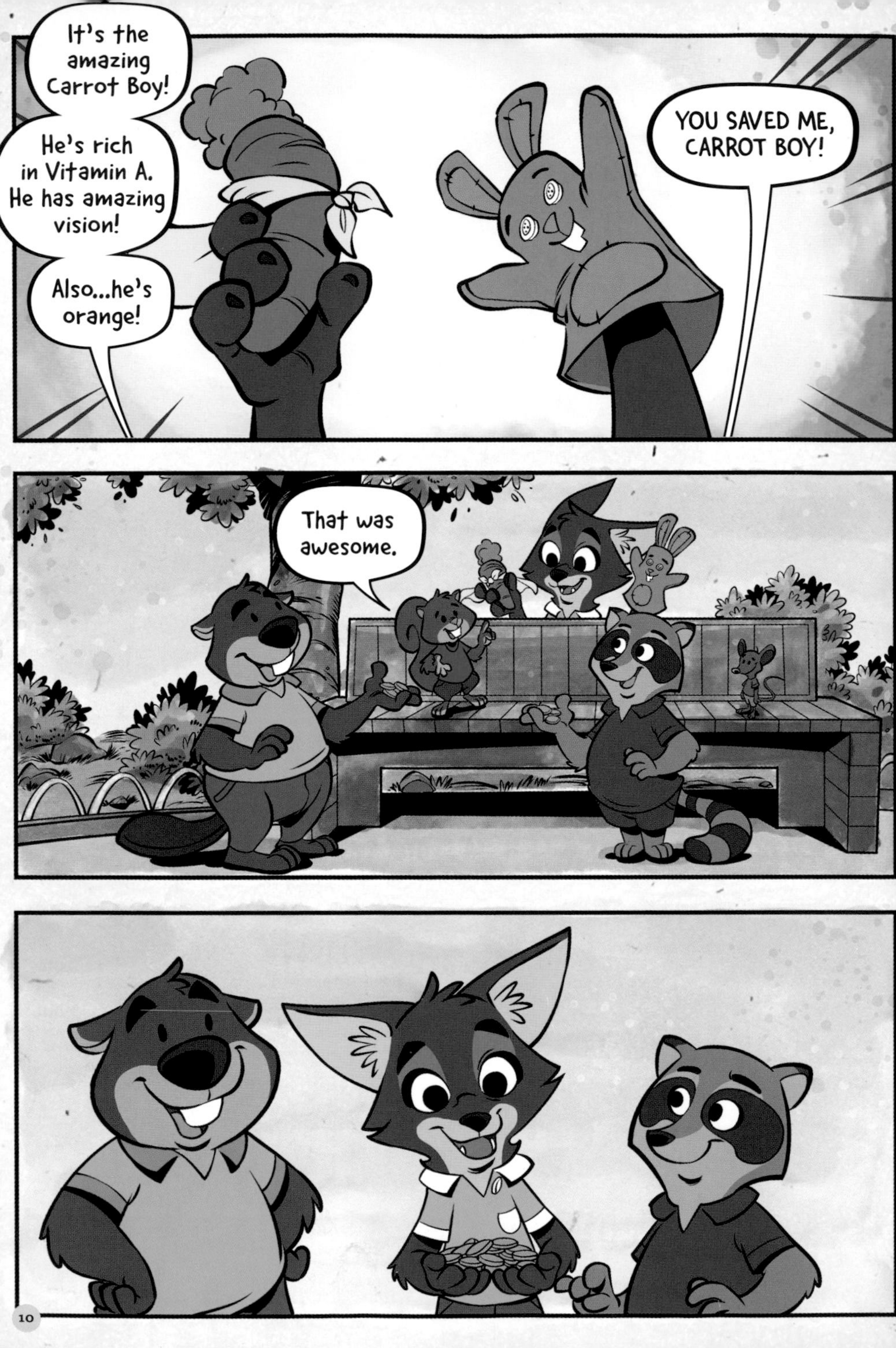
It's the amazing Carrot Boy!
He's rich in Vitamin A. He has amazing vision!
Also...he's orange!
YOU SAVED ME, CARROT BOY!
That was awesome.

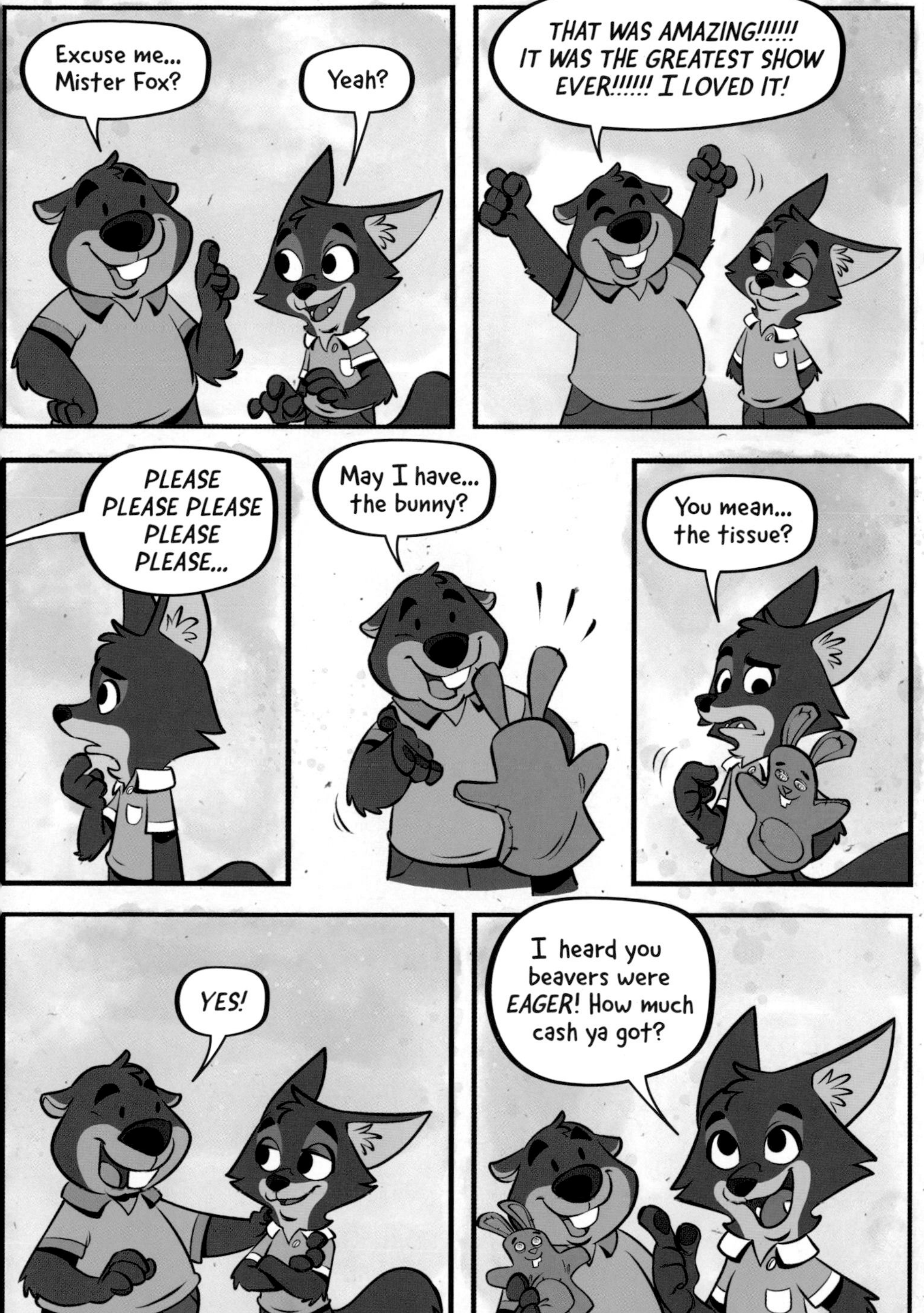

Excuse me... Mister Fox?
Yeah?
THAT WAS AMAZING!!!!!! IT WAS THE GREATEST SHOW EVER!!!!!! I LOVED IT!
PLEASE PLEASE PLEASE PLEASE PLEASE...
May I have... the bunny?
You mean... the tissue?
YES!
I heard you beavers were *EAGER*! How much cash ya got?

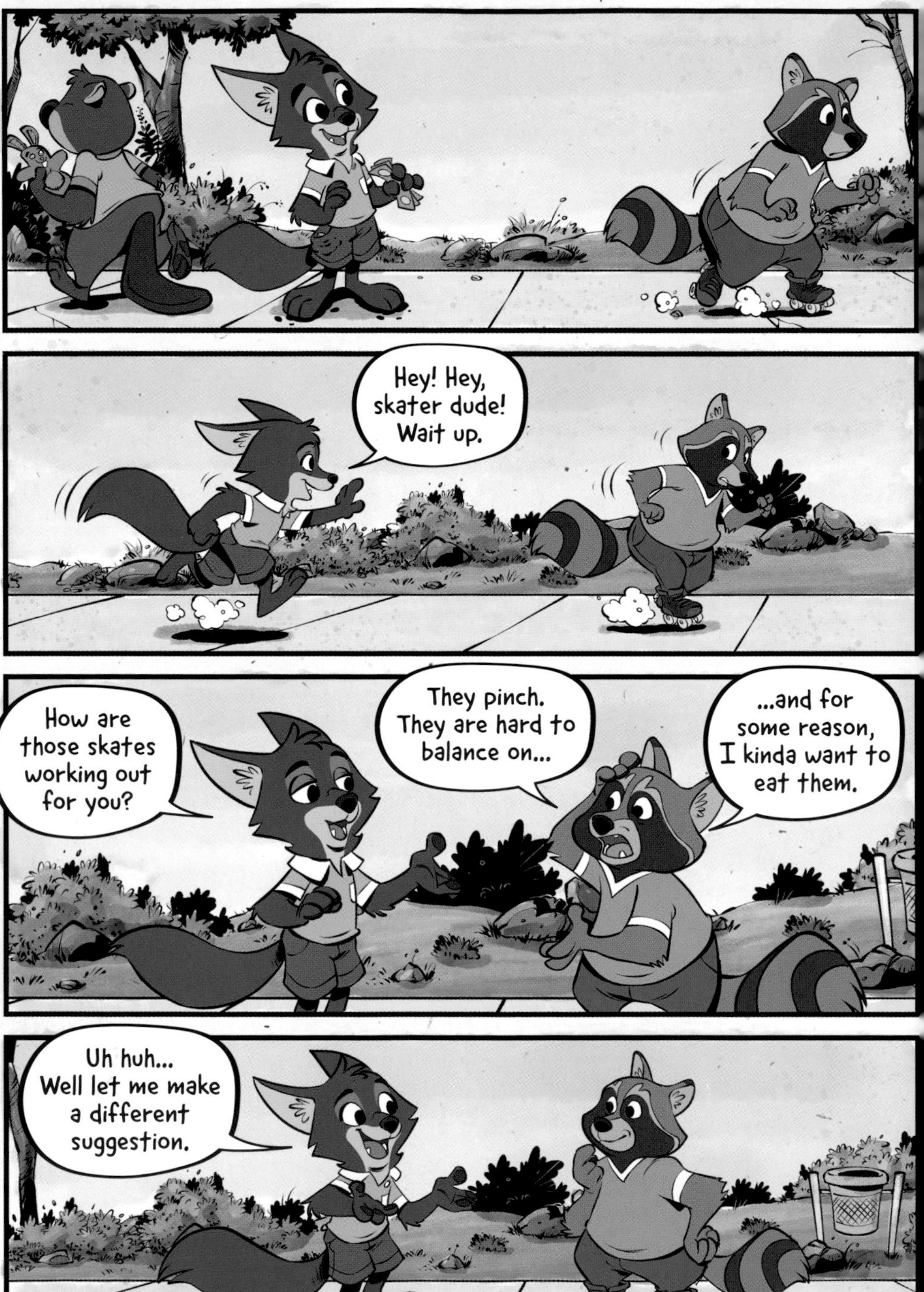

Hey! Hey, skater dude! Wait up.
How are those skates working out for you?
They pinch. They are hard to balance on...
...and for some reason, I kinda want to eat them.
Uh huh... Well let me make a different suggestion.

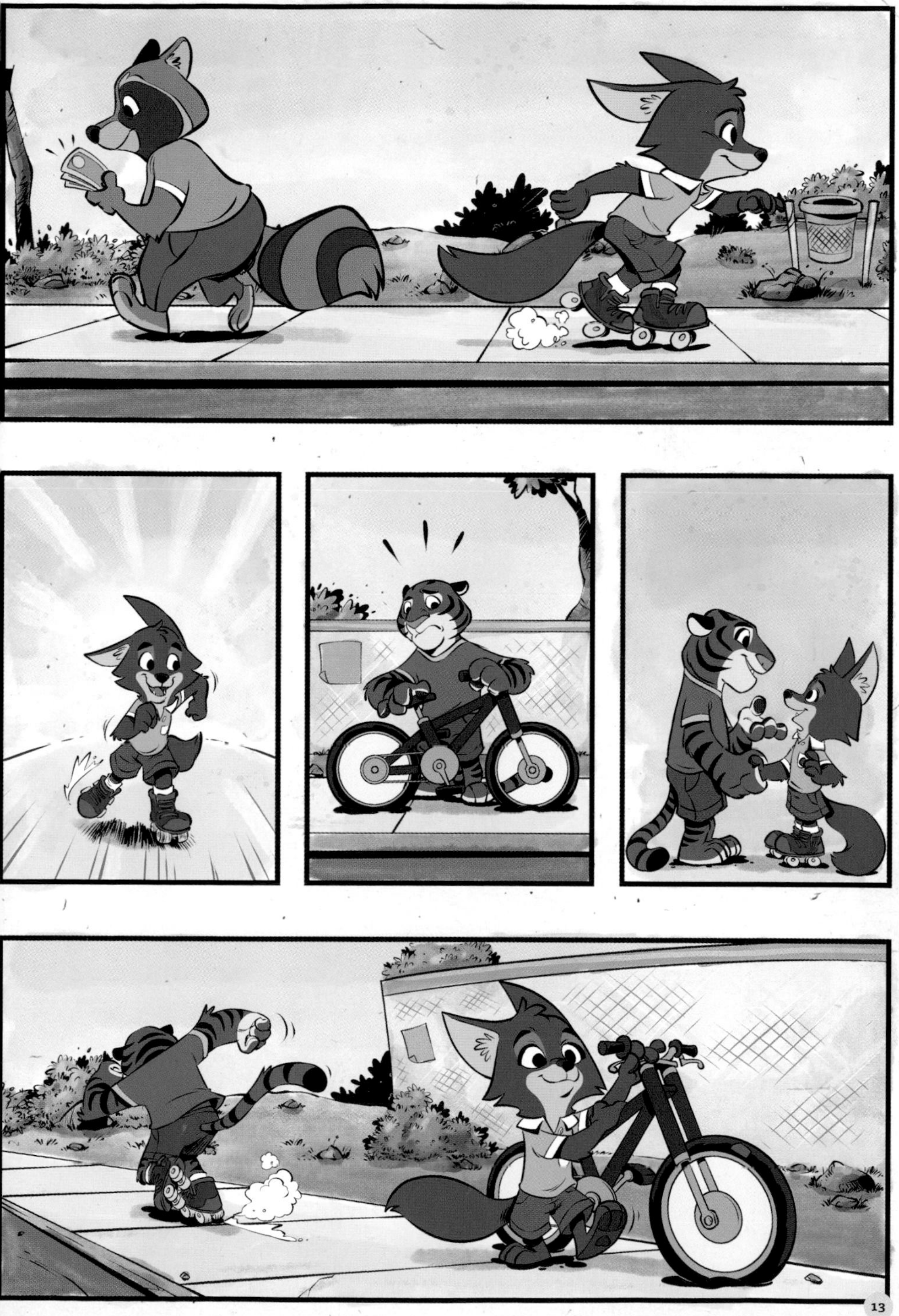

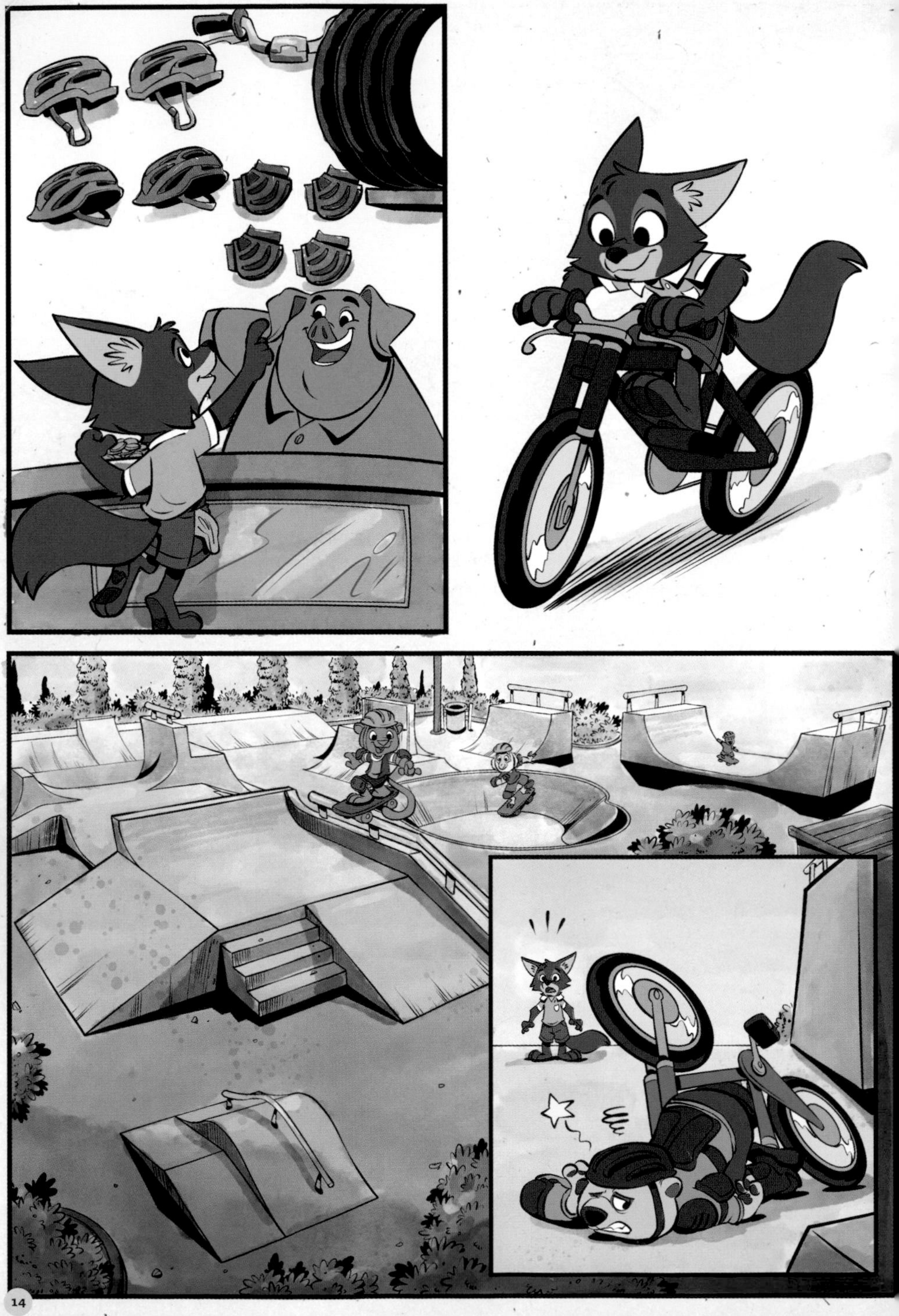

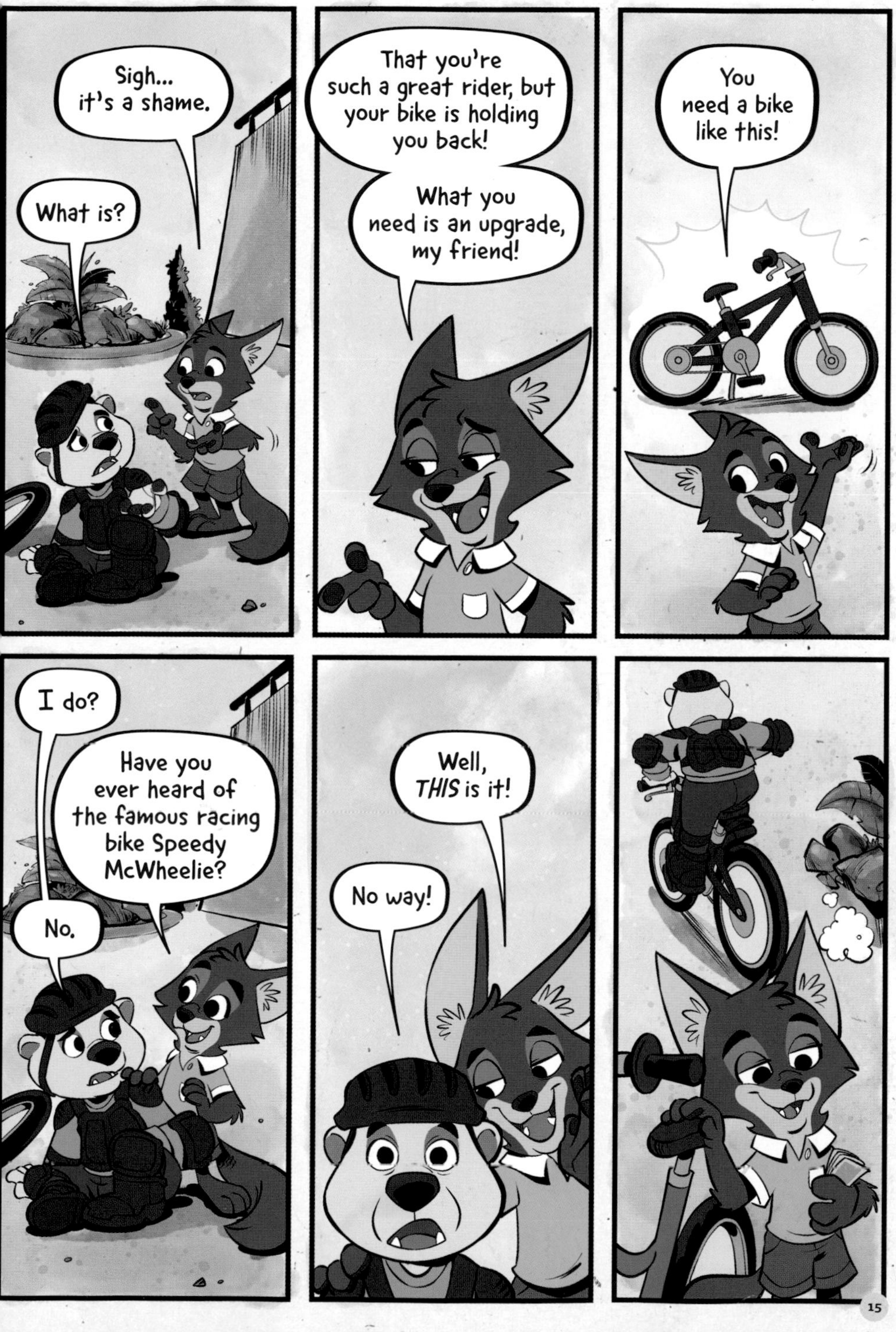
Sigh...
it's a shame.
What is?
That you're
such a great rider, but
your bike is holding
you back!
What you
need is an upgrade,
my friend!
You
need a bike
like this!
I do?
Have you
ever heard of
the famous racing
bike Speedy
McWheelie?
No.
Well,
THIS is it!
No way!

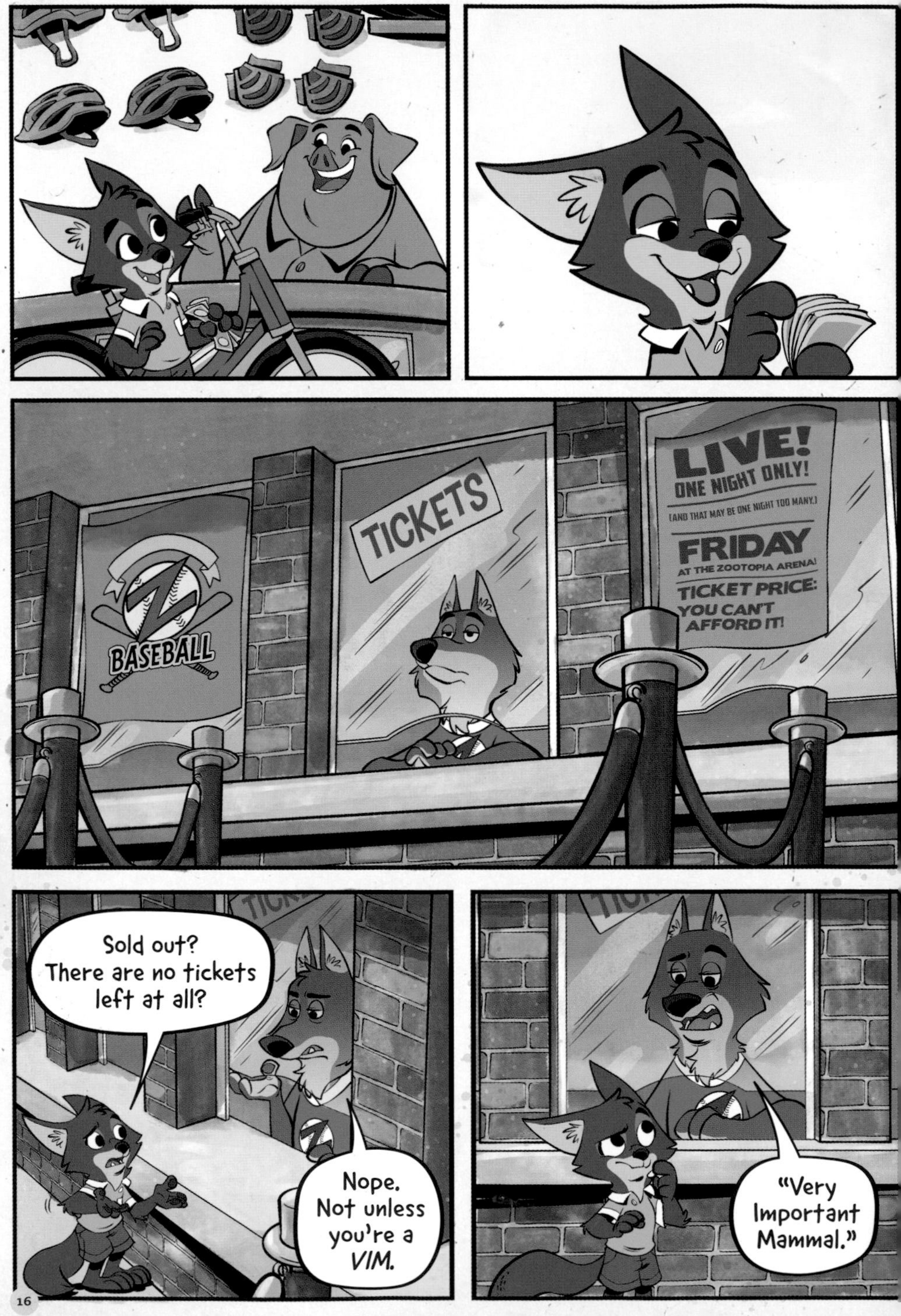
BASEBALL
TICKETS
LIVE!
ONE NIGHT ONLY!
(AND THAT MAY BE ONE NIGHT TOO MANY.)
FRIDAY
AT THE ZOOTOPIA ARENA!
TICKET PRICE:
YOU CAN'T AFFORD IT!
Sold out? There are no tickets left at all?
Nope. Not unless you're a *VIM*.
"Very Important Mammal."

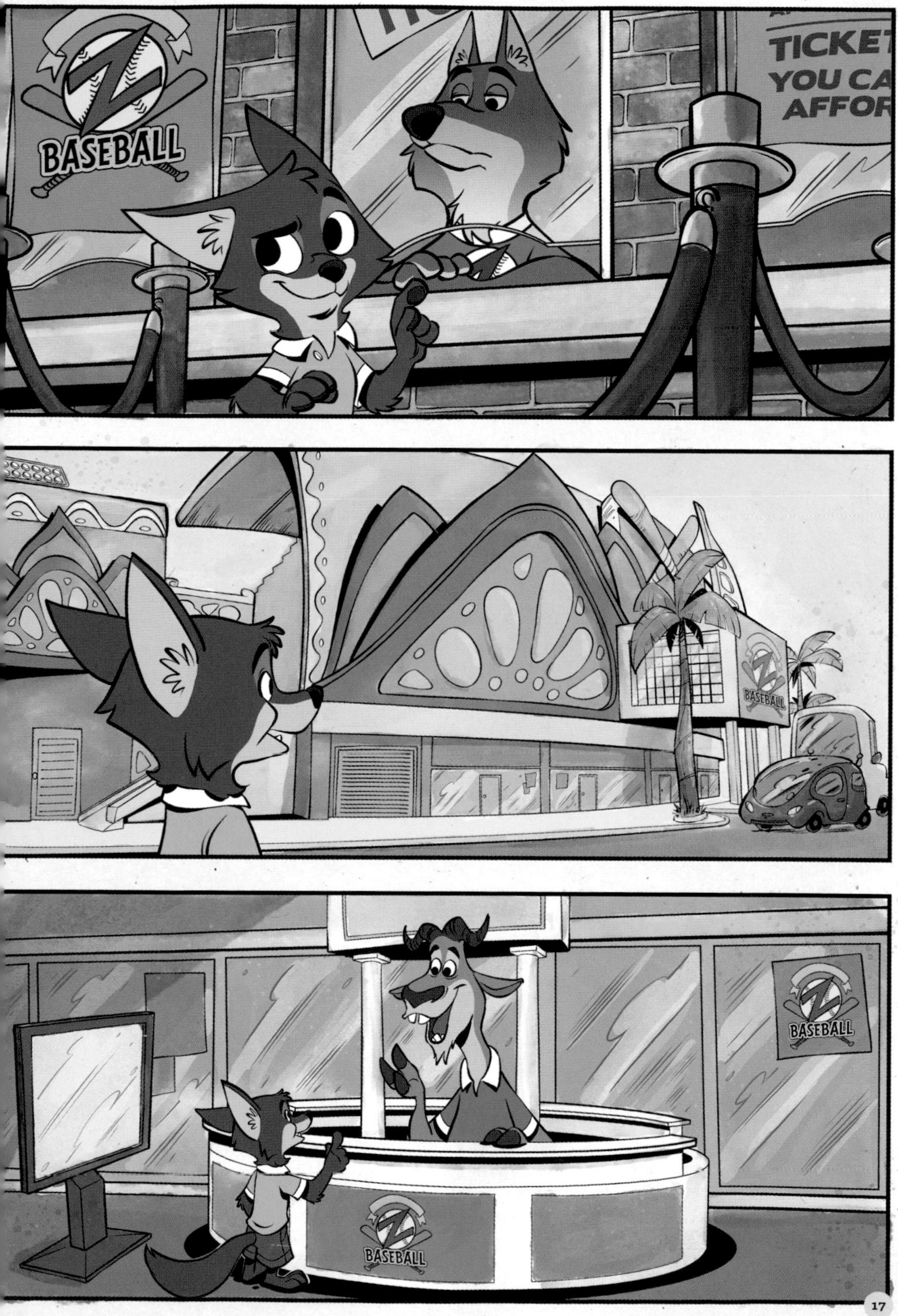
BASEBALL
BASEBALL
BASEBALL
BASEBALL

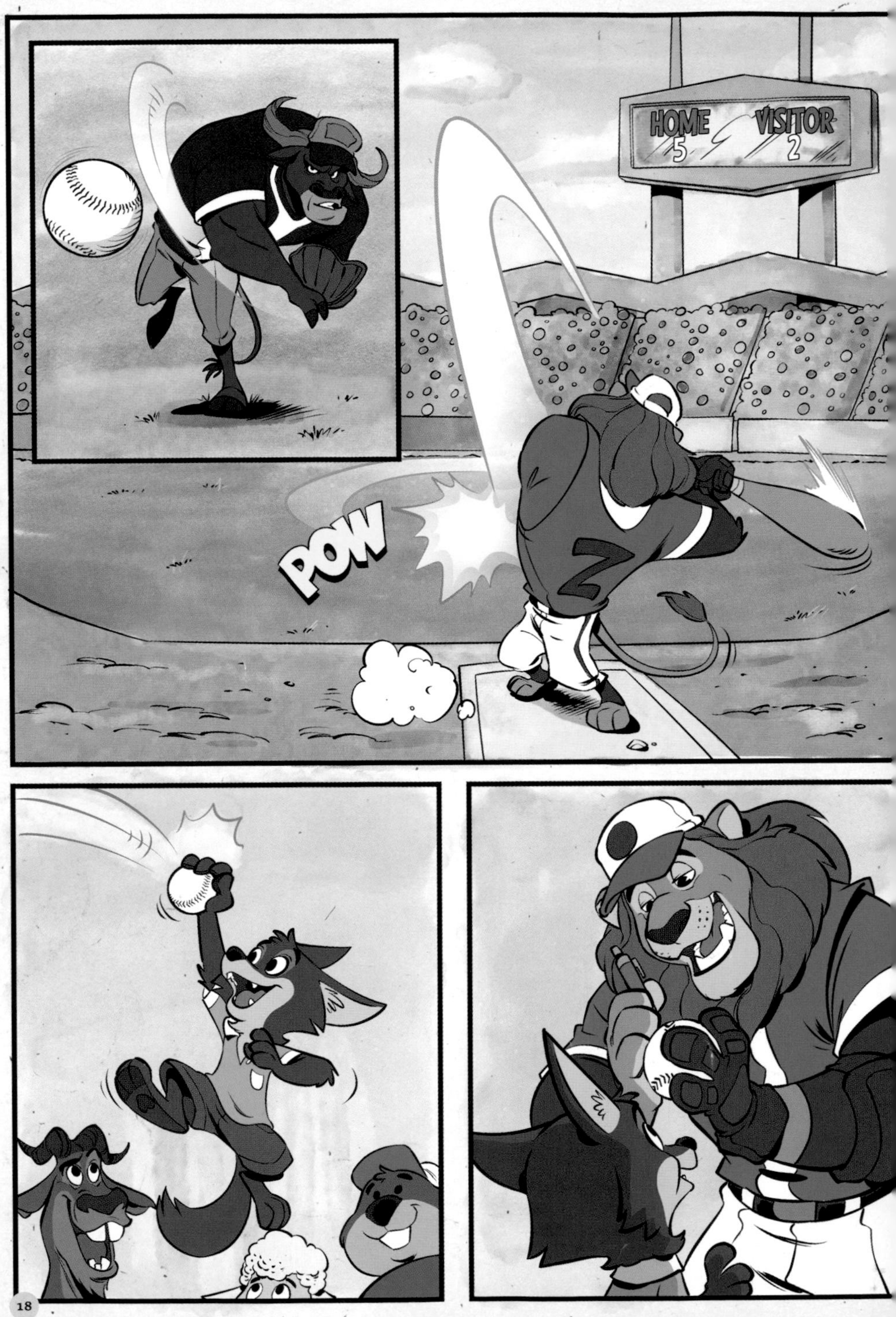
HOME 5
VISITOR 2
POW

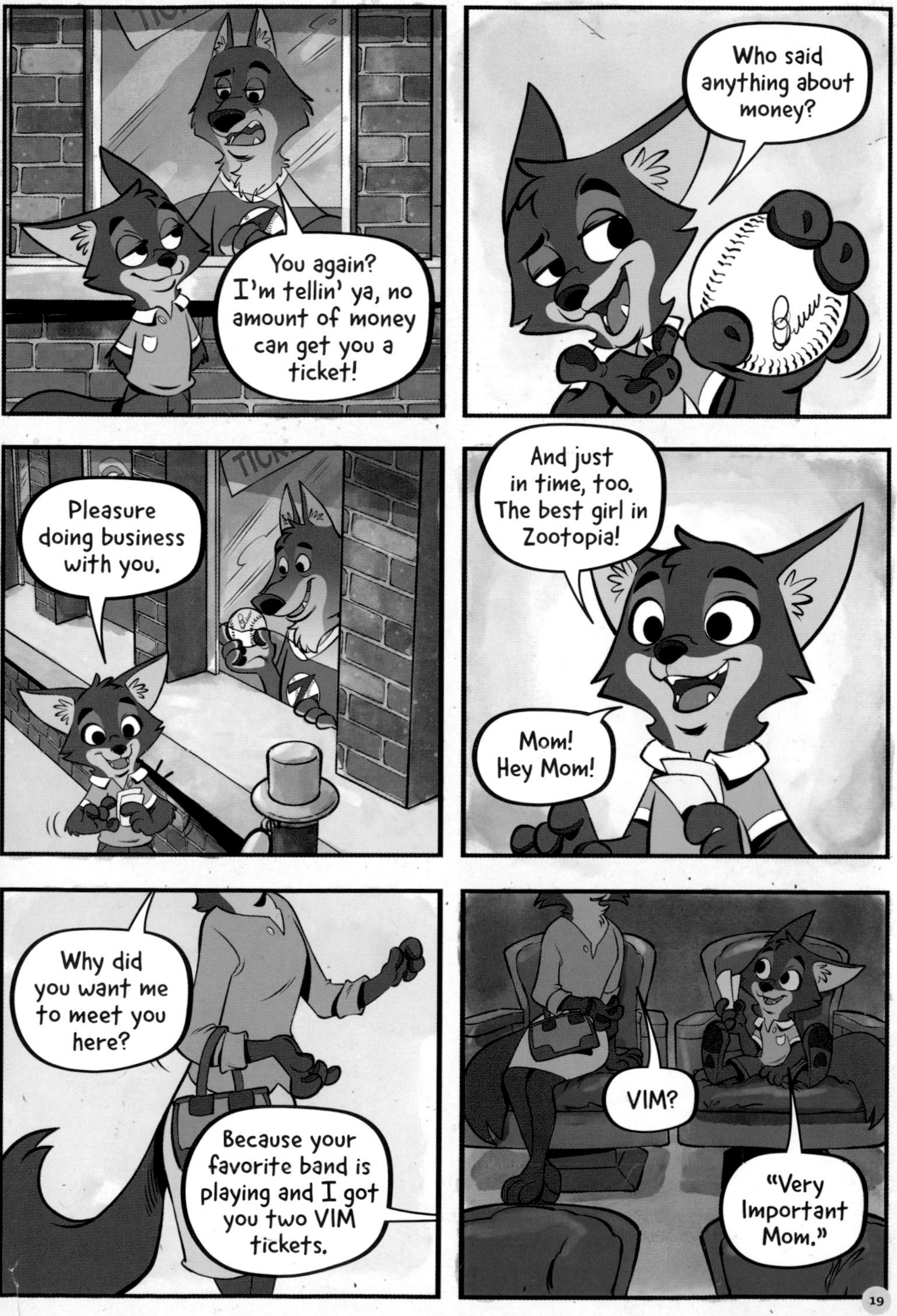
You again? I'm tellin' ya, no amount of money can get you a ticket!
Who said anything about money?
Pleasure doing business with you.
And just in time, too. The best girl in Zootopia!
Mom! Hey Mom!
Why did you want me to meet you here?
Because your favorite band is playing and I got you two VIM tickets.
VIM?
"Very Important Mom."

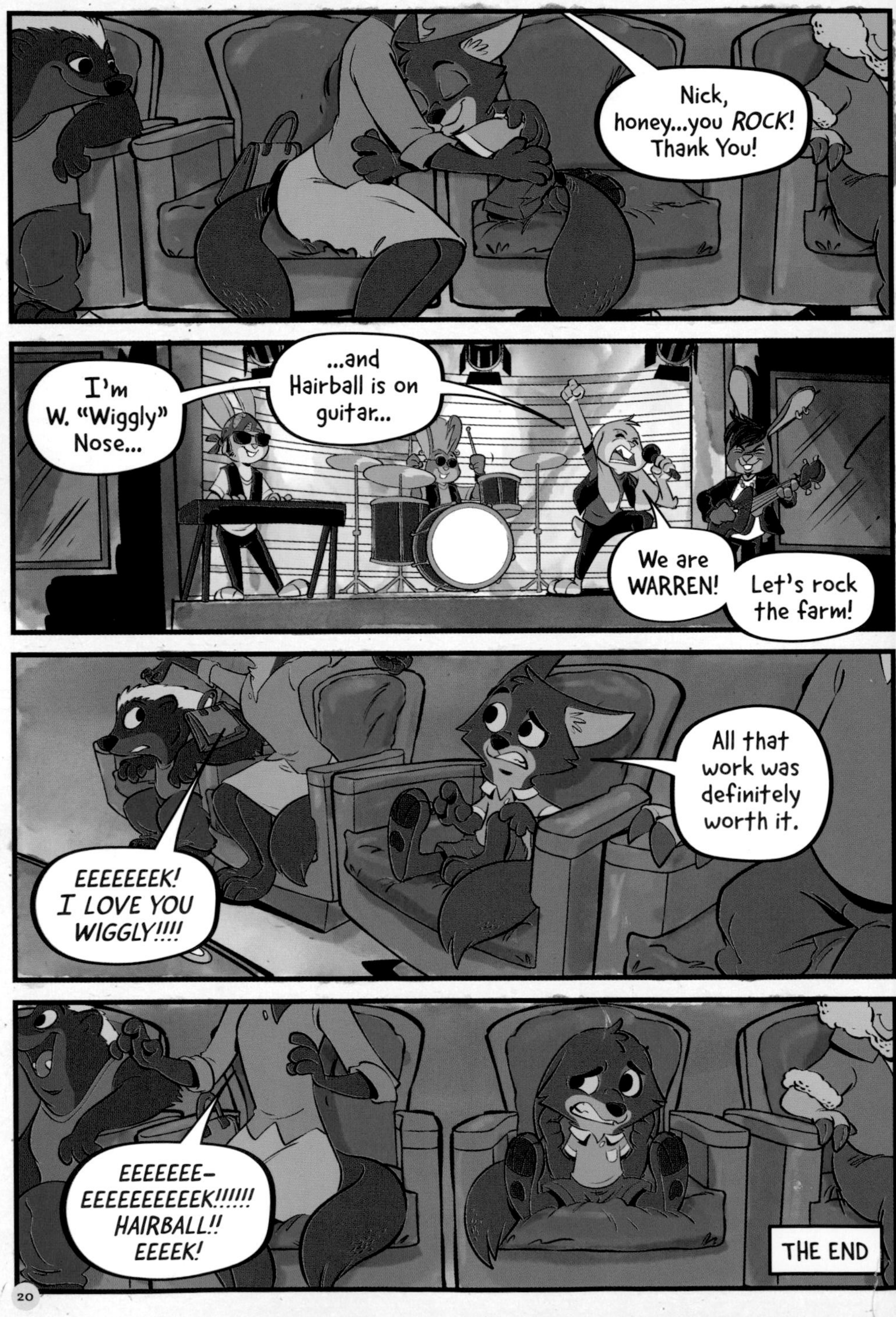
Nick, honey...you ROCK! Thank You!
I'm W. "Wiggly" Nose...
...and Hairball is on guitar...
We are WARREN!
Let's rock the farm!
All that work was definitely worth it.
EEEEEEEK! I LOVE YOU WIGGLY!!!!
EEEEEEE-EEEEEEEEEK!!!!!! HAIRBALL!! EEEEK!
THE END

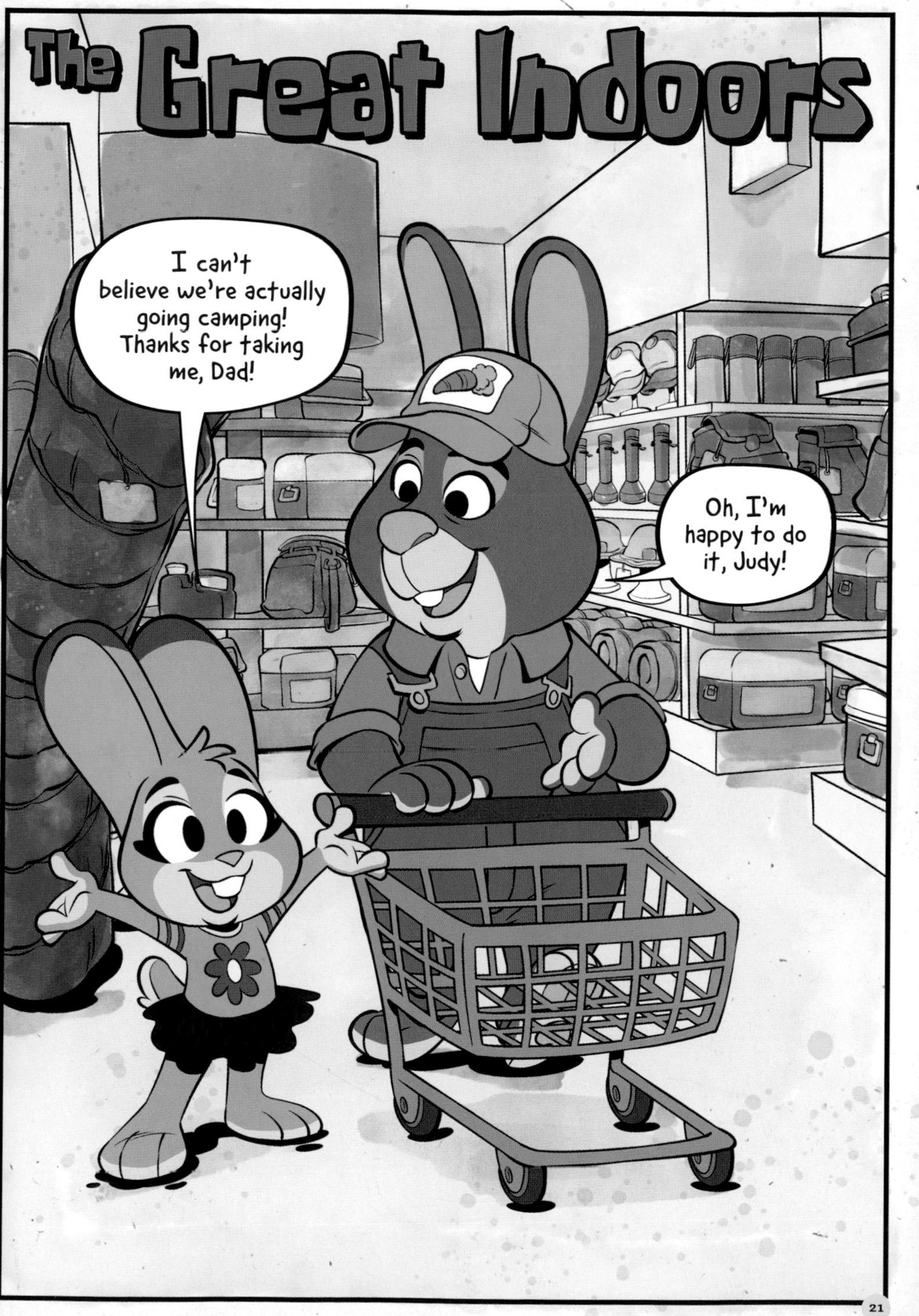
The Great Indoors
I can't believe we're actually going camping! Thanks for taking me, Dad!
Oh, I'm happy to do it, Judy!

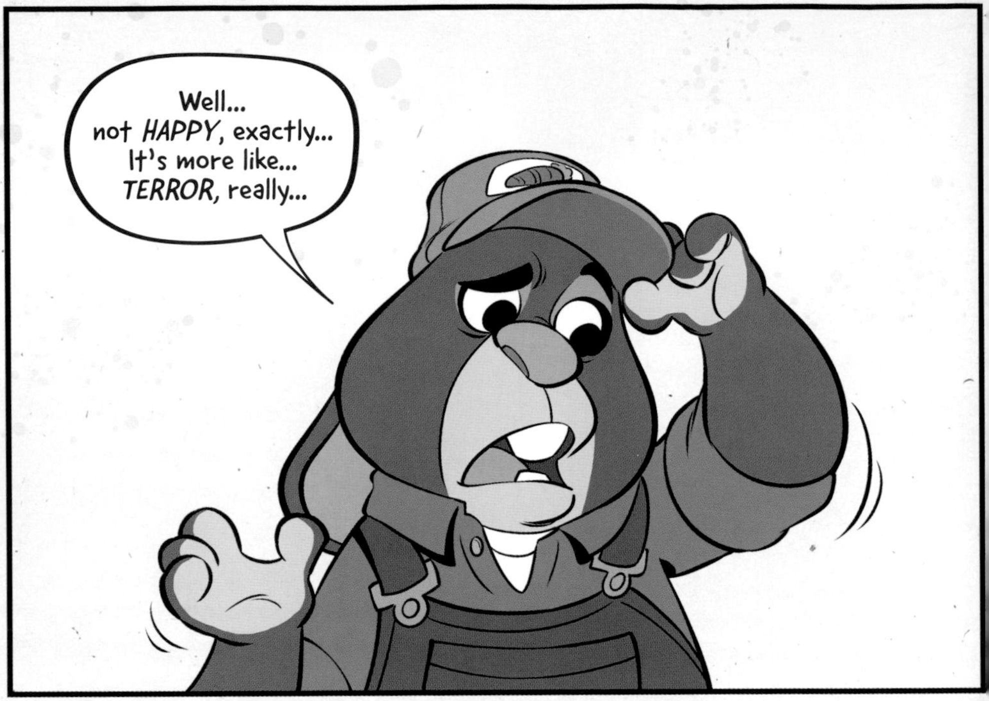
Well... not *HAPPY*, exactly... It's more like... *TERROR*, really...

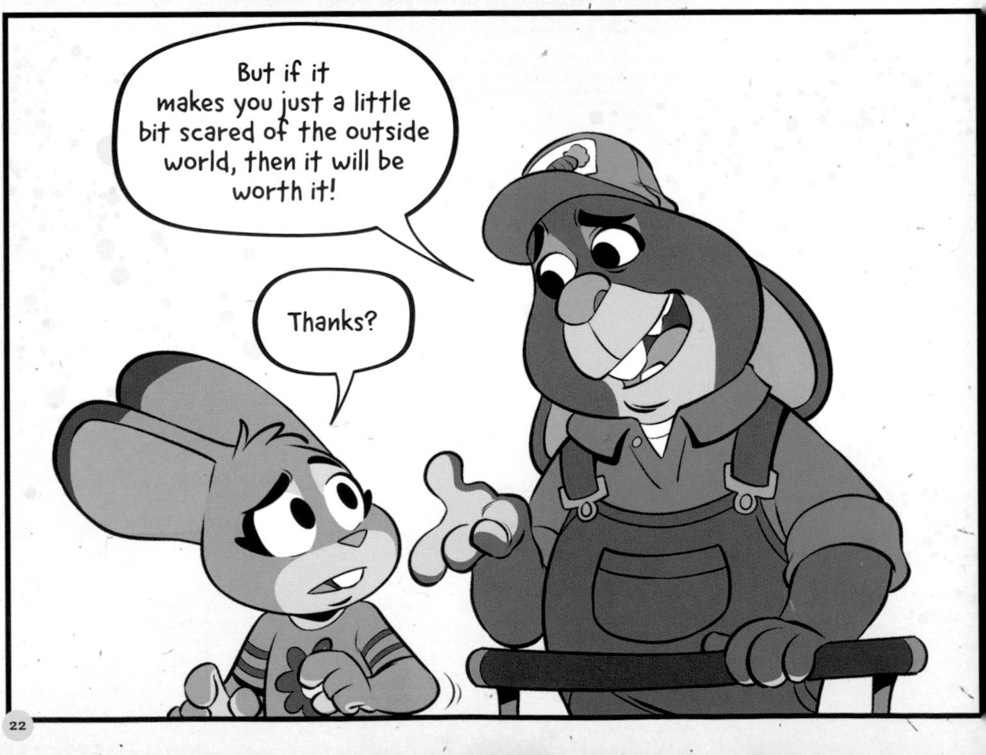
But if it makes you just a little bit scared of the outside world, then it will be worth it!
Thanks?

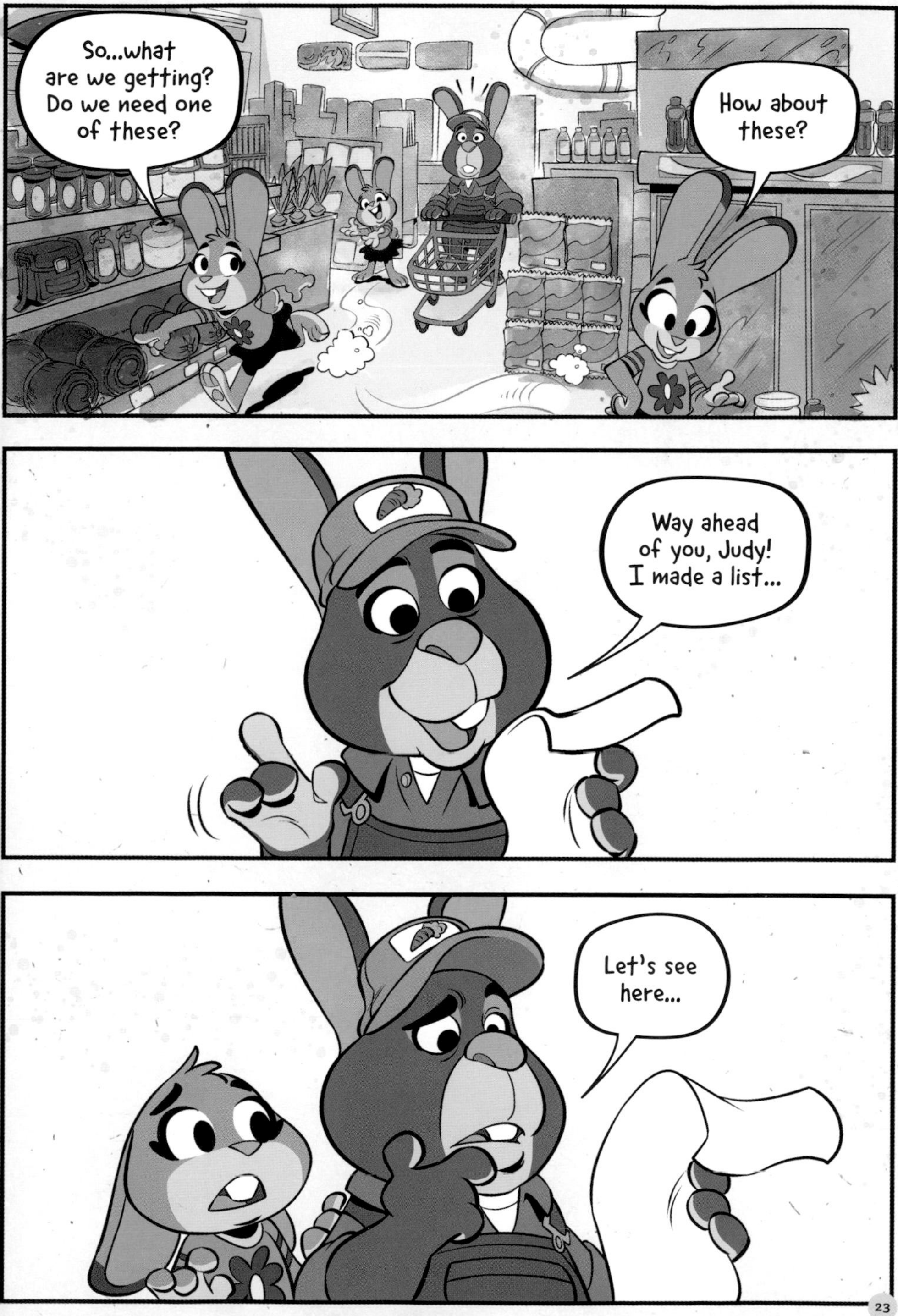

So...what are we getting? Do we need one of these?
How about these?
Way ahead of you, Judy! I made a list...
Let's see here...

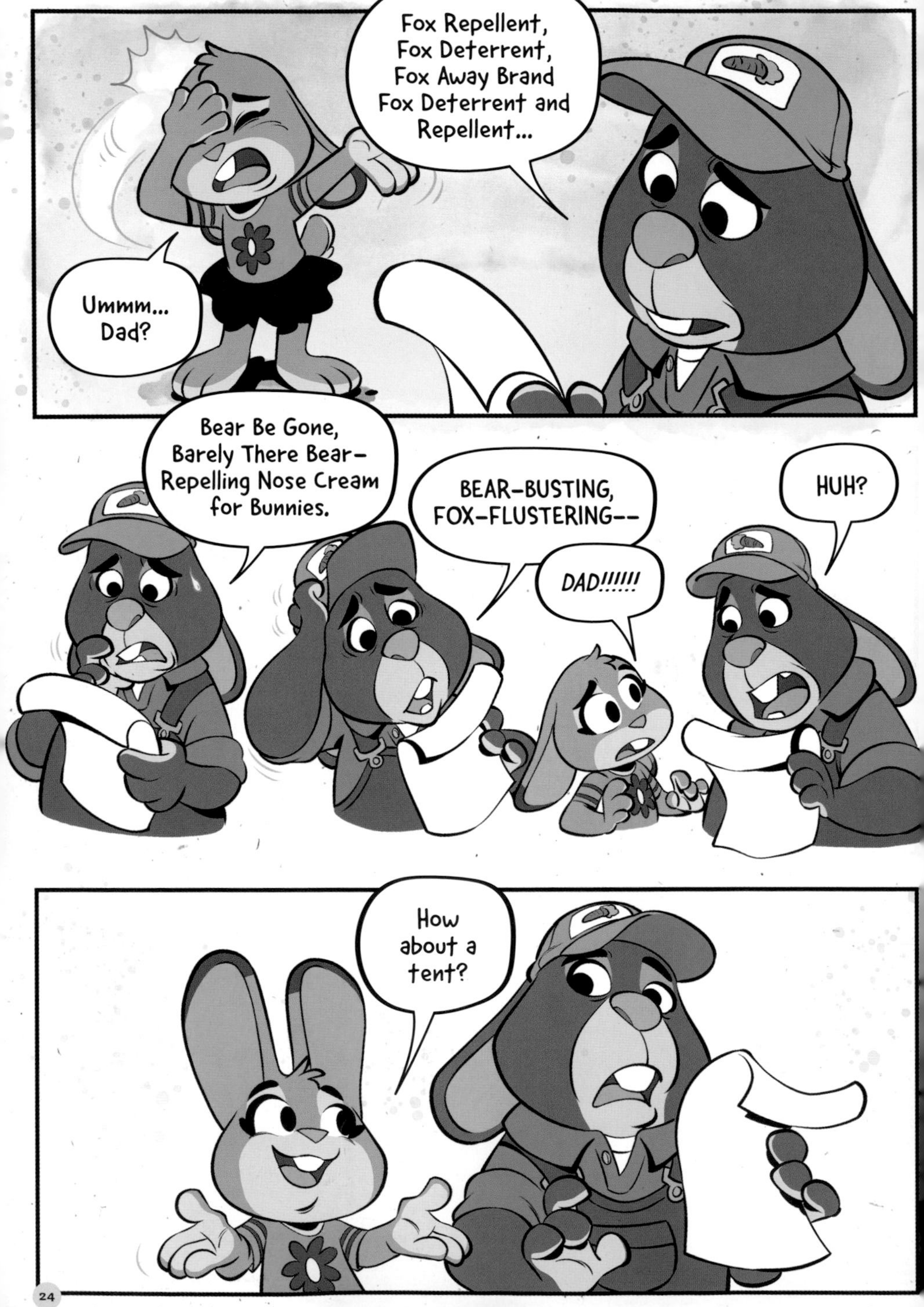
Fox Repellent, Fox Deterrent, Fox Away Brand Fox Deterrent and Repellent...
Ummm... Dad?
Bear Be Gone, Barely There Bear-Repelling Nose Cream for Bunnies.
BEAR-BUSTING, FOX-FLUSTERING--
DAD!!!!!!
HUH?
How about a tent?

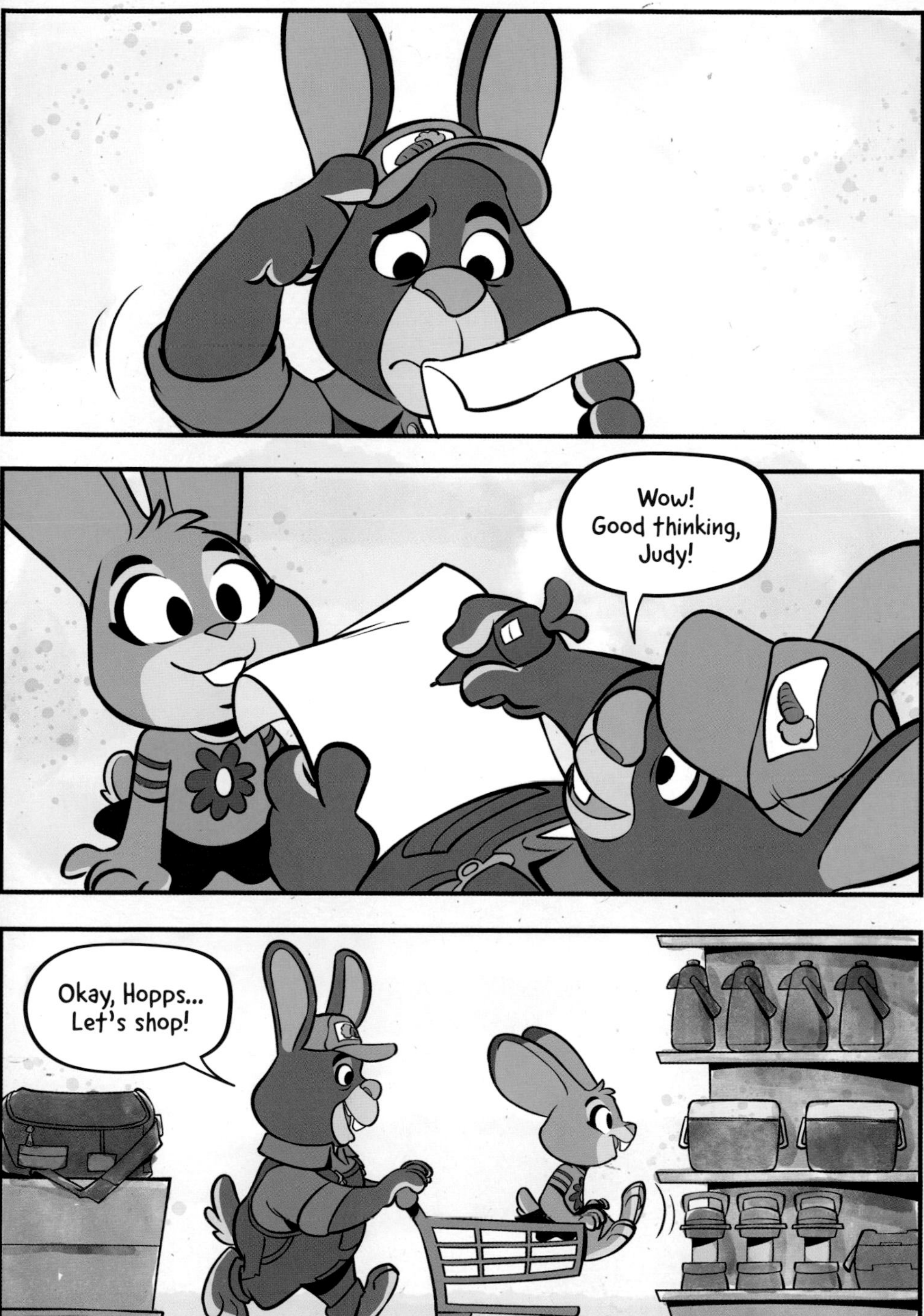
Wow! Good thinking, Judy!
Okay, Hopps... Let's shop!

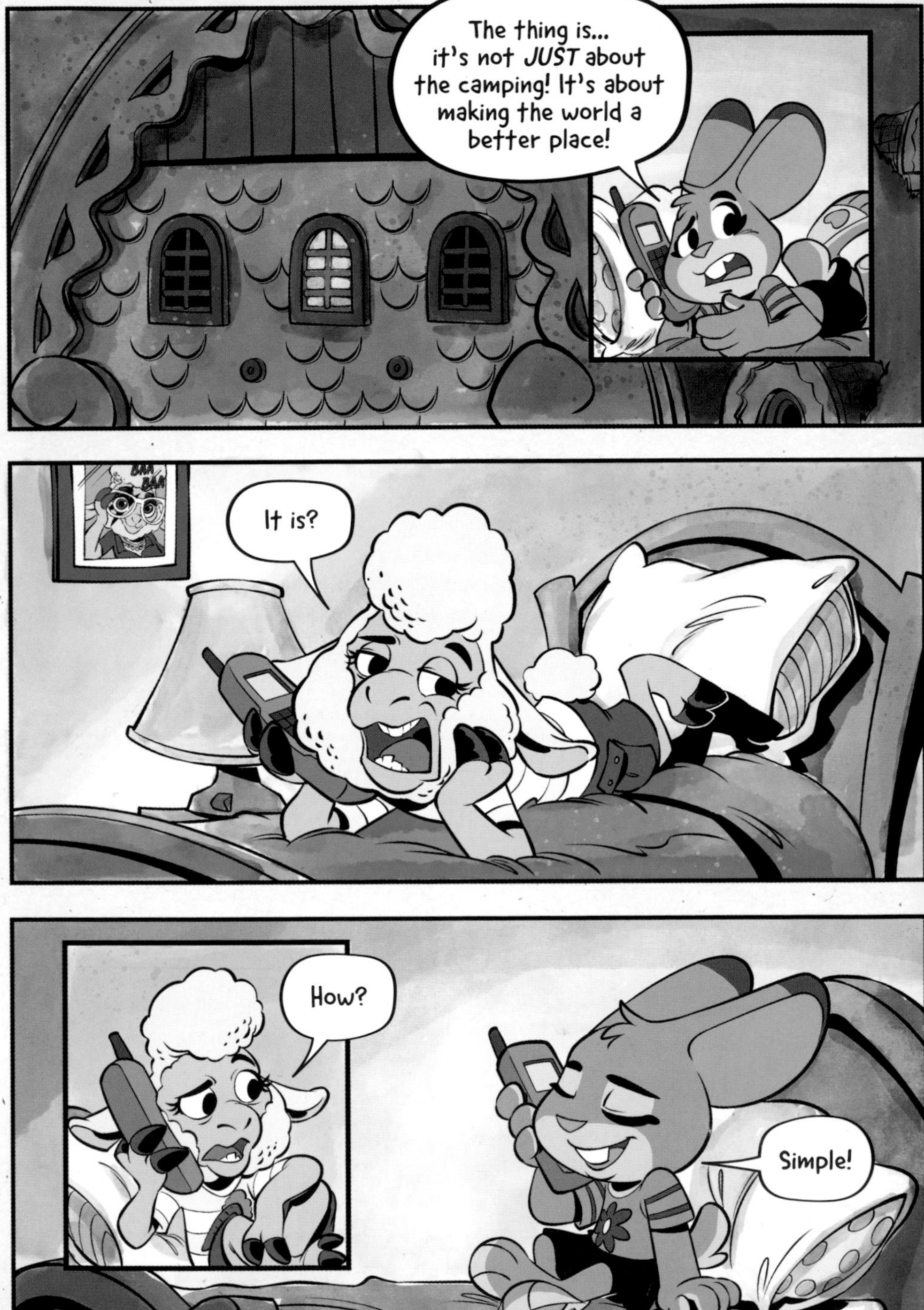
The thing is... it's not JUST about the camping! It's about making the world a better place!
It is?
How?
Simple!

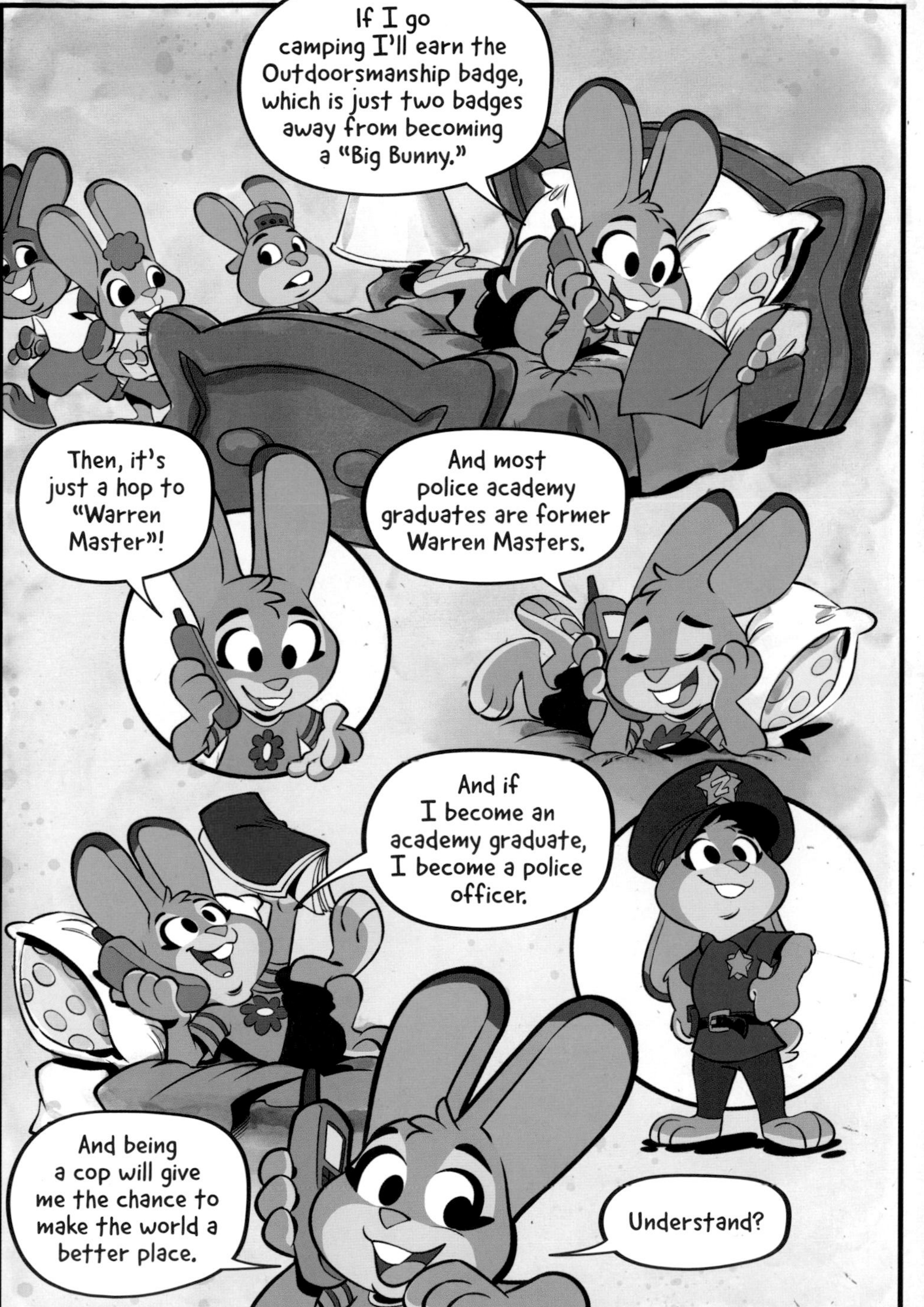
If I go camping I'll earn the Outdoorsmanship badge, which is just two badges away from becoming a "Big Bunny."
Then, it's just a hop to "Warren Master"!
And most police academy graduates are former Warren Masters.
And if I become an academy graduate, I become a police officer.
And being a cop will give me the chance to make the world a better place.
Understand?

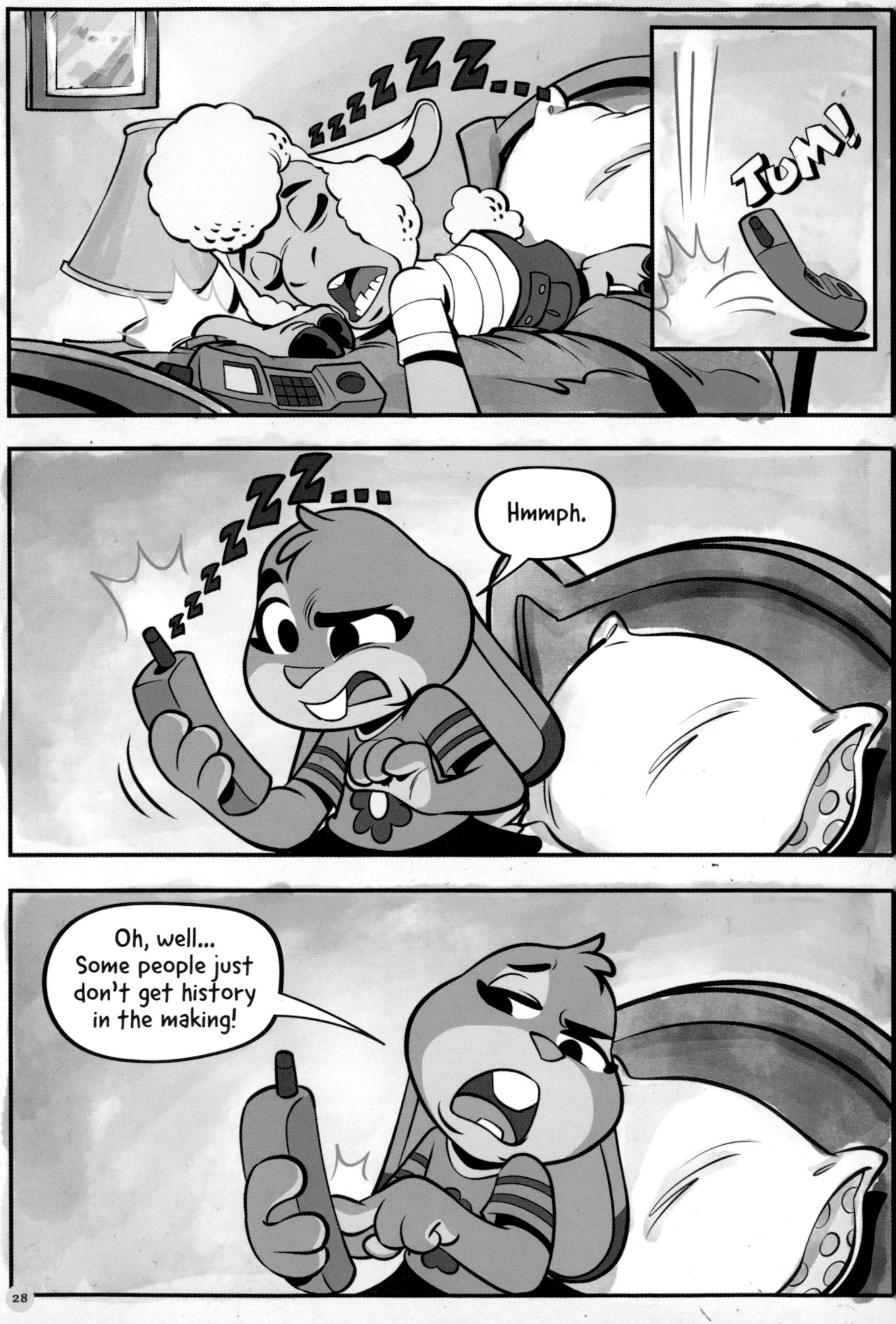

zzzZZZ...
TUM!
ZZZZZZ...
Hmmph.
Oh, well...
Some people just
don't get history
in the making!

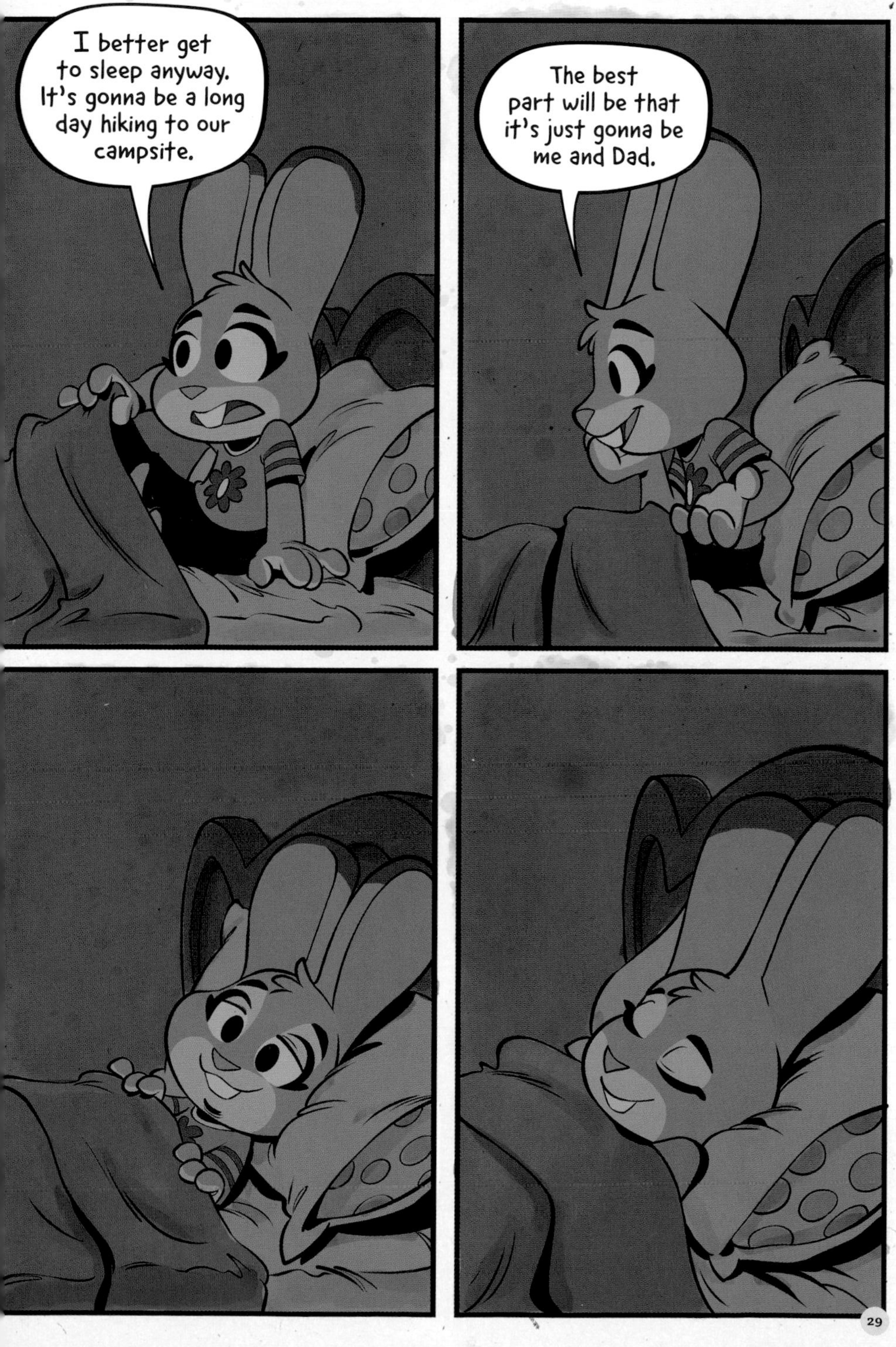
I better get to sleep anyway. It's gonna be a long day hiking to our campsite.
The best part will be that it's just gonna be me and Dad.

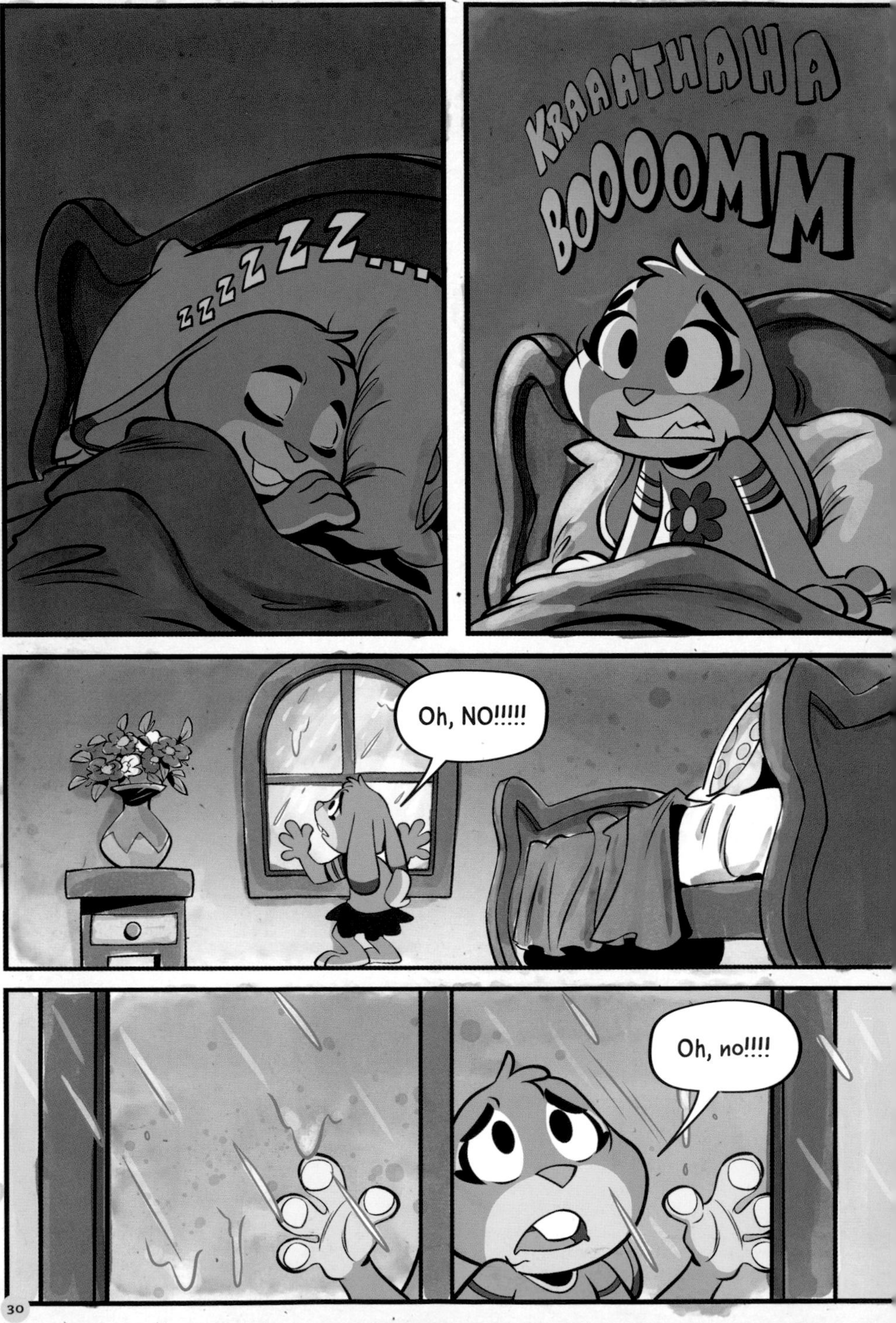
zzzZZZ....
KRAAATHAHA
BOOOOMM
Oh, NO!!!!!
Oh, no!!!!

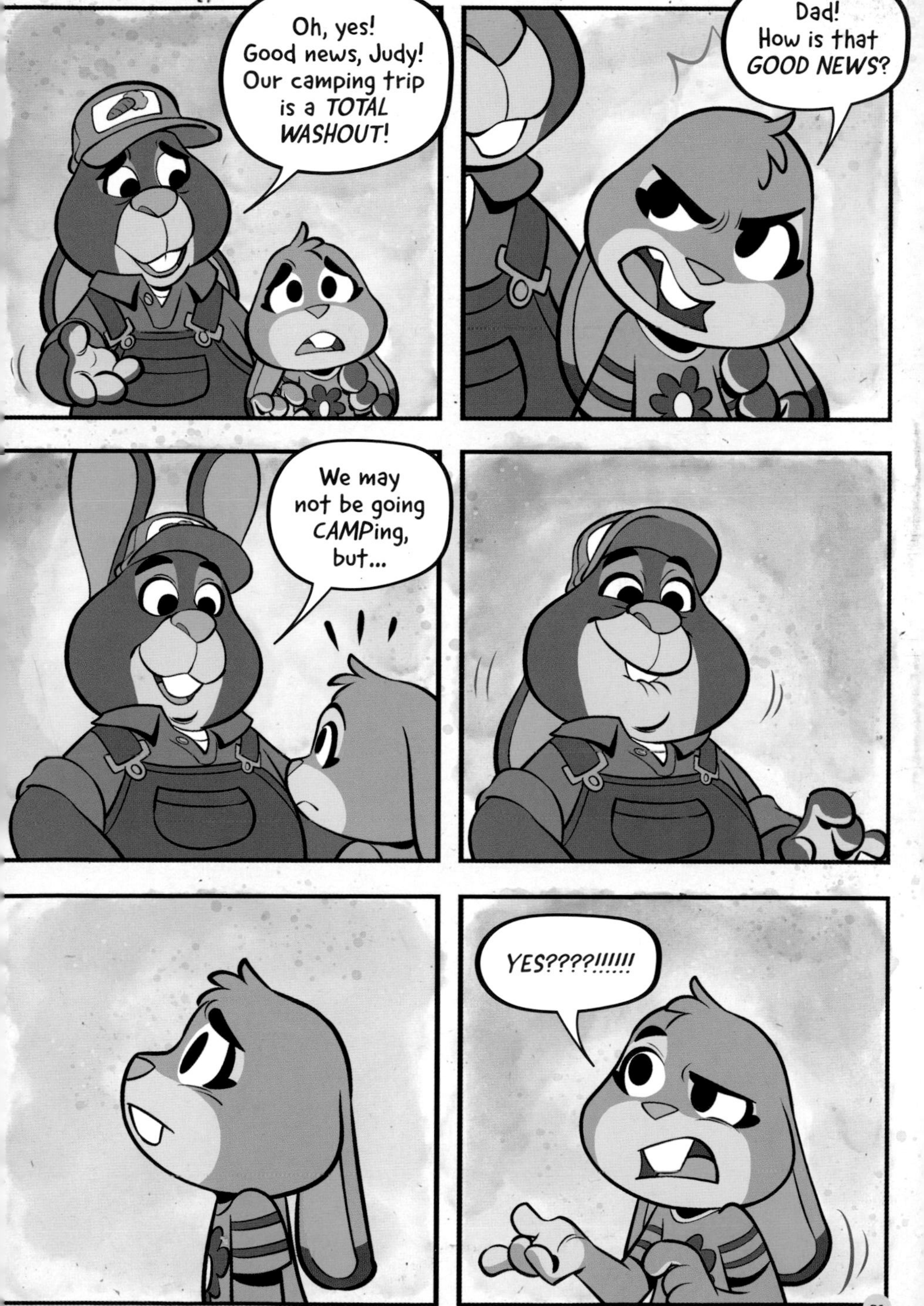
Oh, yes! Good news, Judy! Our camping trip is a TOTAL WASHOUT!
Dad! How is that GOOD NEWS?
We may not be going CAMPing, but...
YES????!!!!!!

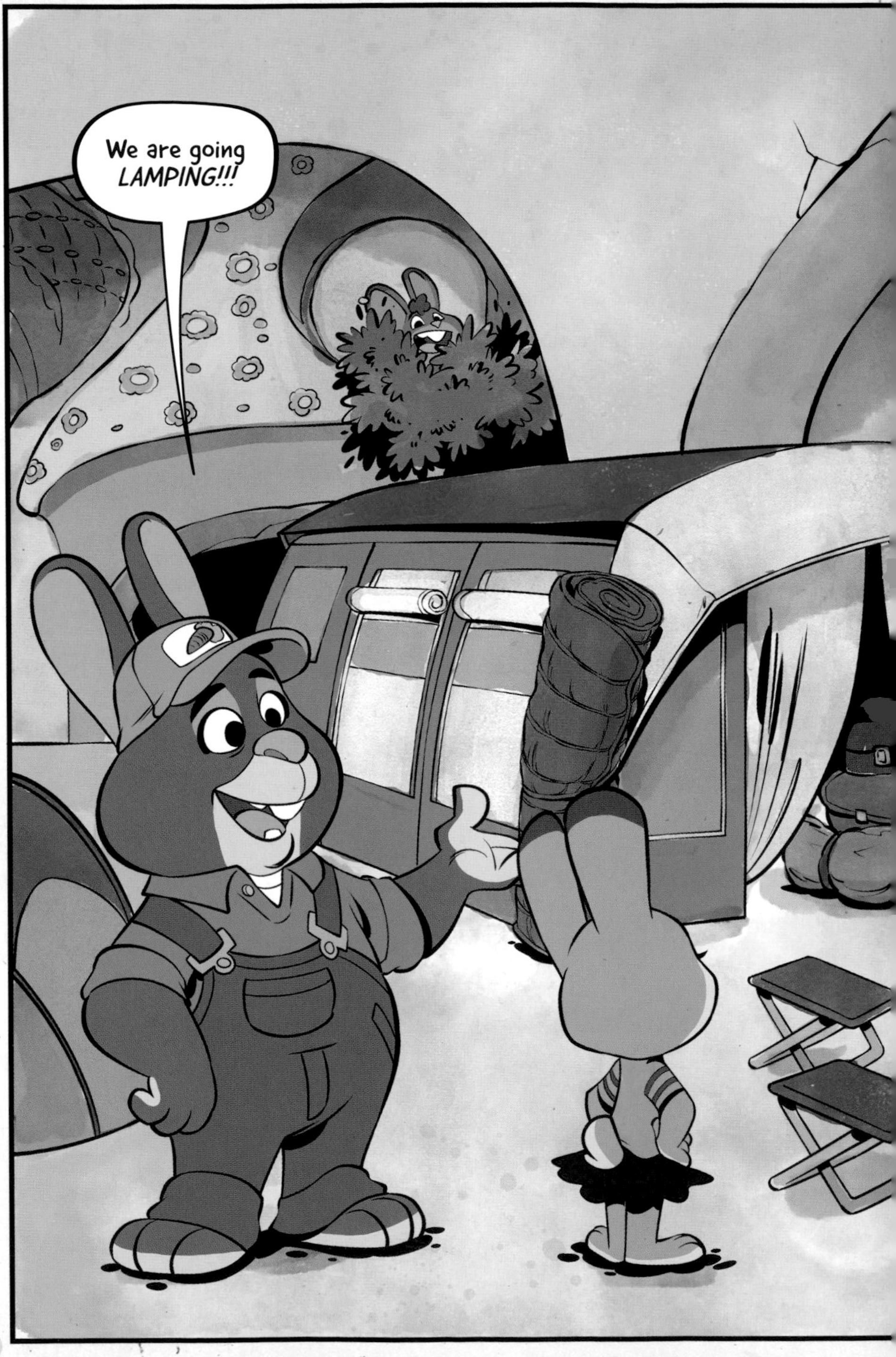
We are going *LAMPING!!!*

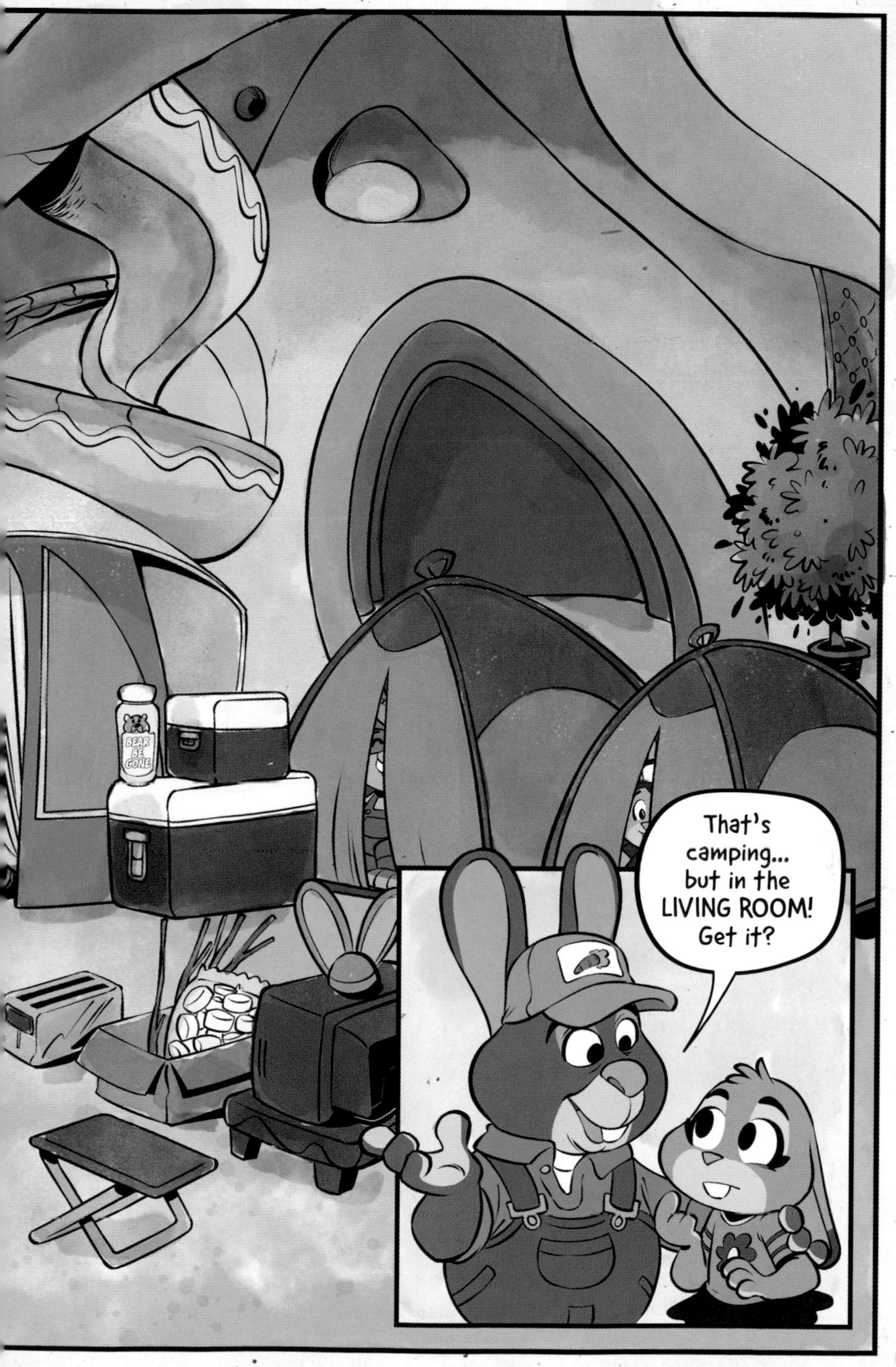
BEAR BE GONE
That's camping... but in the LIVING ROOM! Get it?

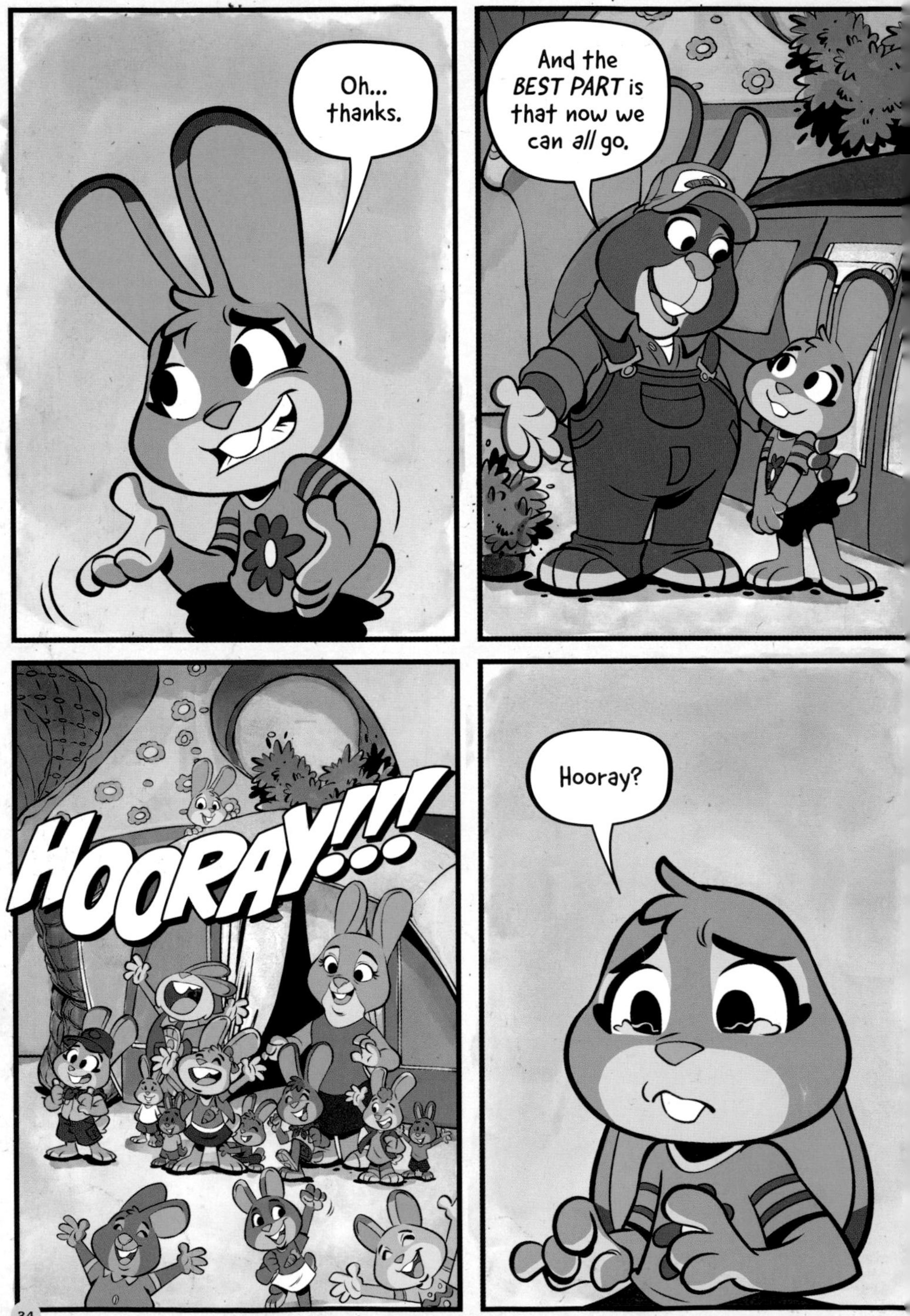

Oh... thanks.
And the *BEST PART* is that now we can *all* go.
HOORAY!!!
Hooray?

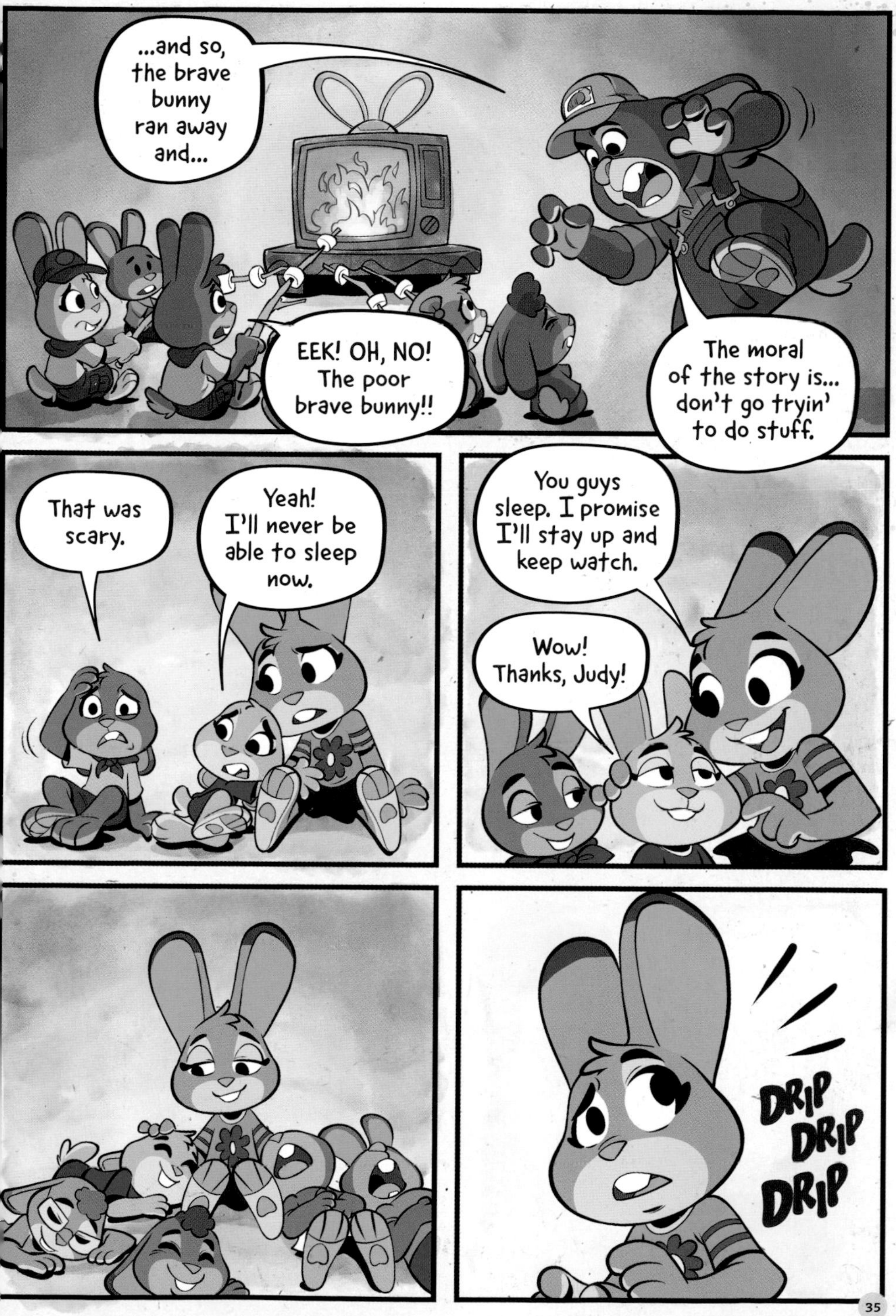
...and so, the brave bunny ran away and...
EEK! OH, NO! The poor brave bunny!!
The moral of the story is... don't go tryin' to do stuff.
That was scary.
Yeah! I'll never be able to sleep now.
You guys sleep. I promise I'll stay up and keep watch.
Wow! Thanks, Judy!
DRIP DRIP DRIP

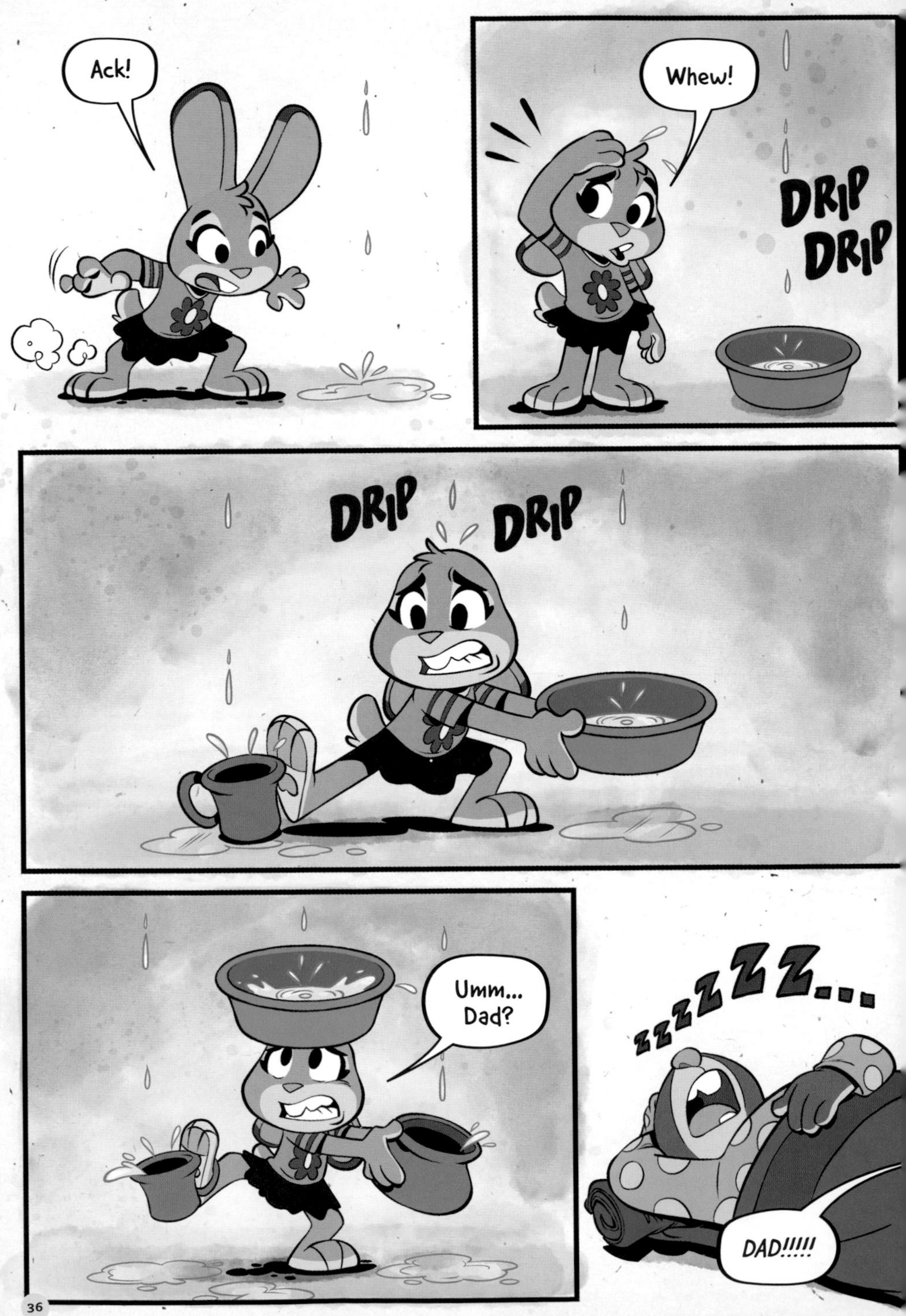
Ack!
Whew!
DRIP
DRIP
DRIP
DRIP
Umm... Dad?
zzzZZZ...
DAD!!!!!

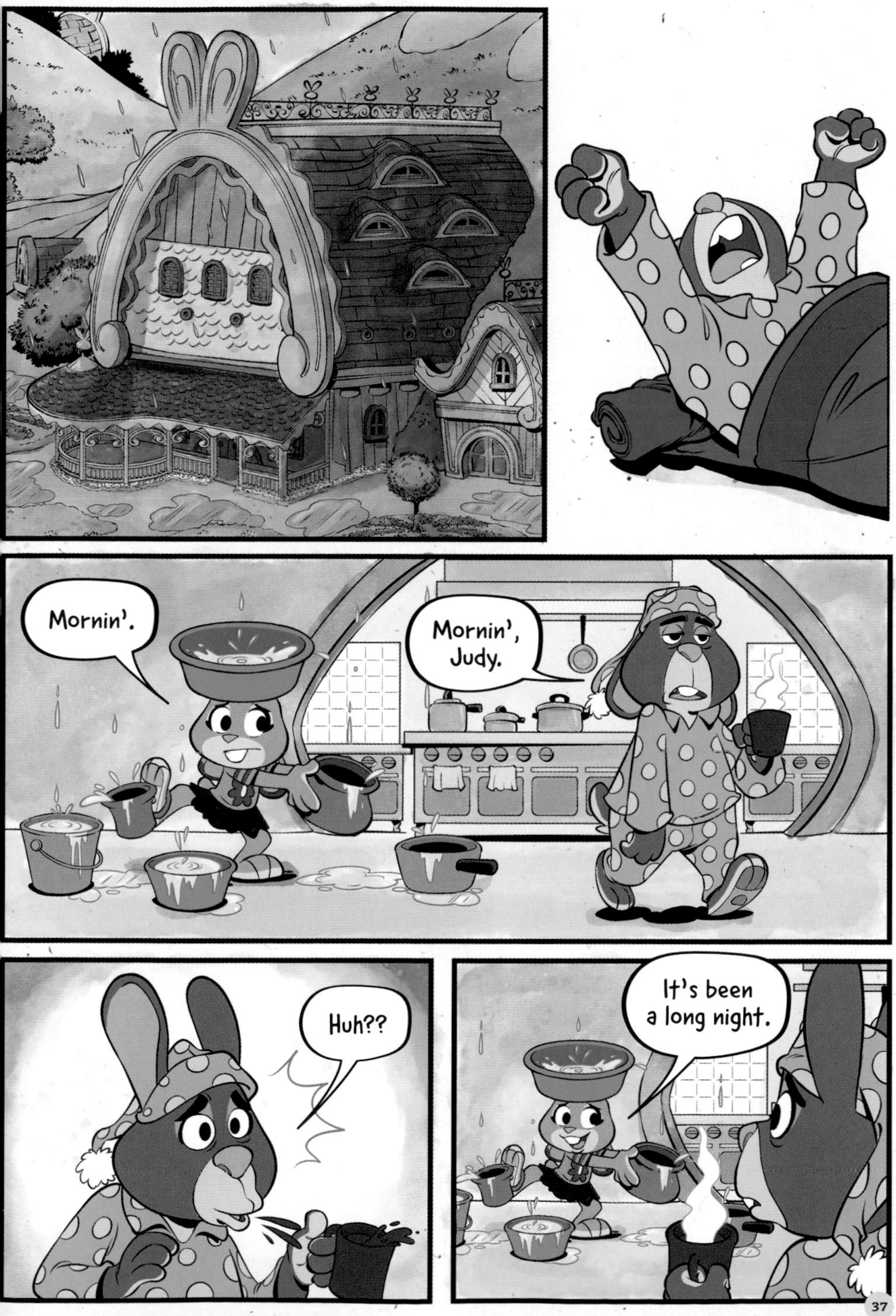
Mornin'.
Mornin', Judy.
Huh??
It's been a long night.

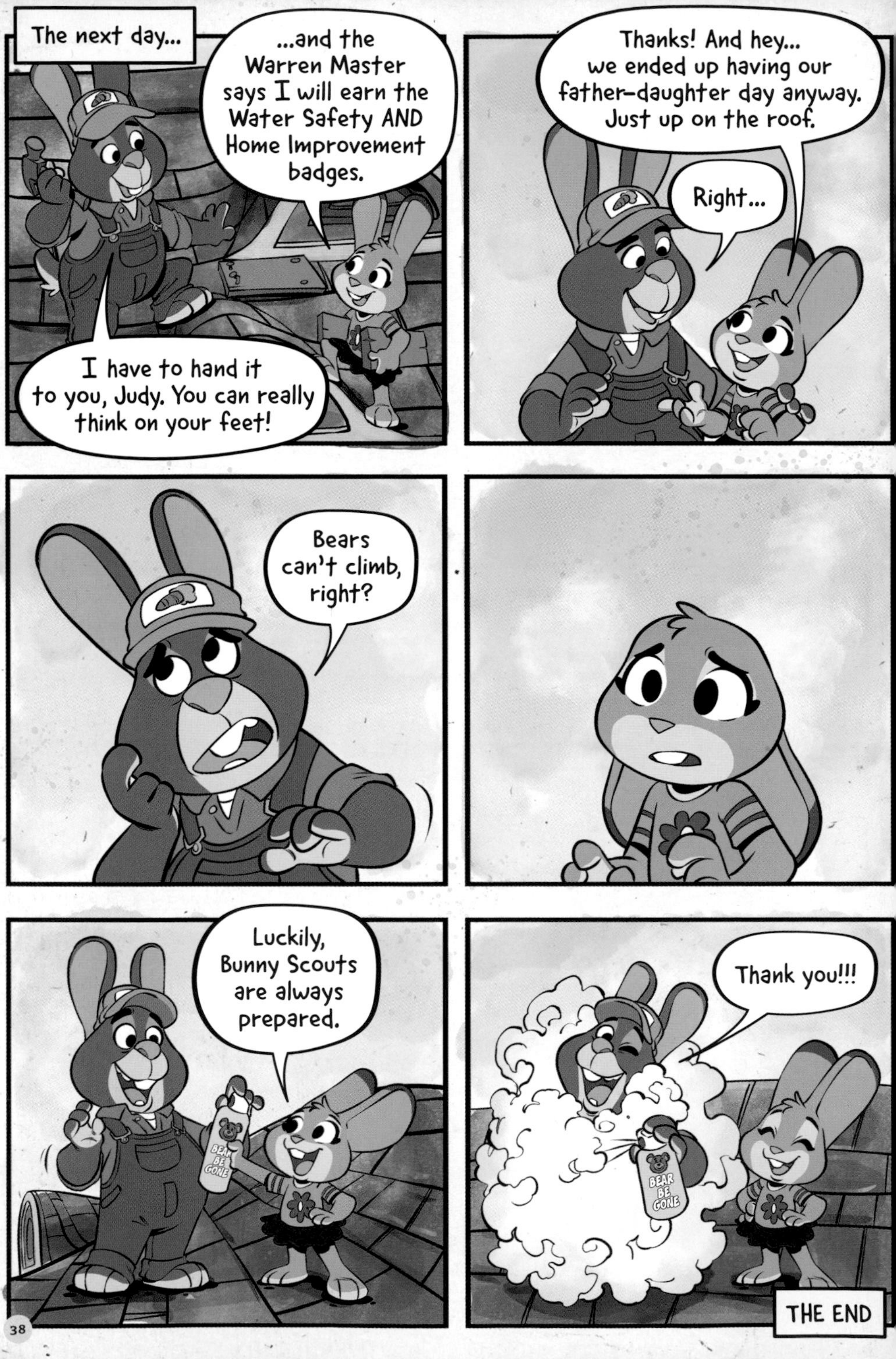
The next day...
...and the Warren Master says I will earn the Water Safety AND Home Improvement badges.
I have to hand it to you, Judy. You can really think on your feet!
Thanks! And hey... we ended up having our father-daughter day anyway. Just up on the roof.
Right...
Bears can't climb, right?
Luckily, Bunny Scouts are always prepared.
BEAR BE GONE
Thank you!!!
BEAR BE GONE
THE END

A MEDLEY OF ACTIVITIES FOR FEROCIOUS FUN!

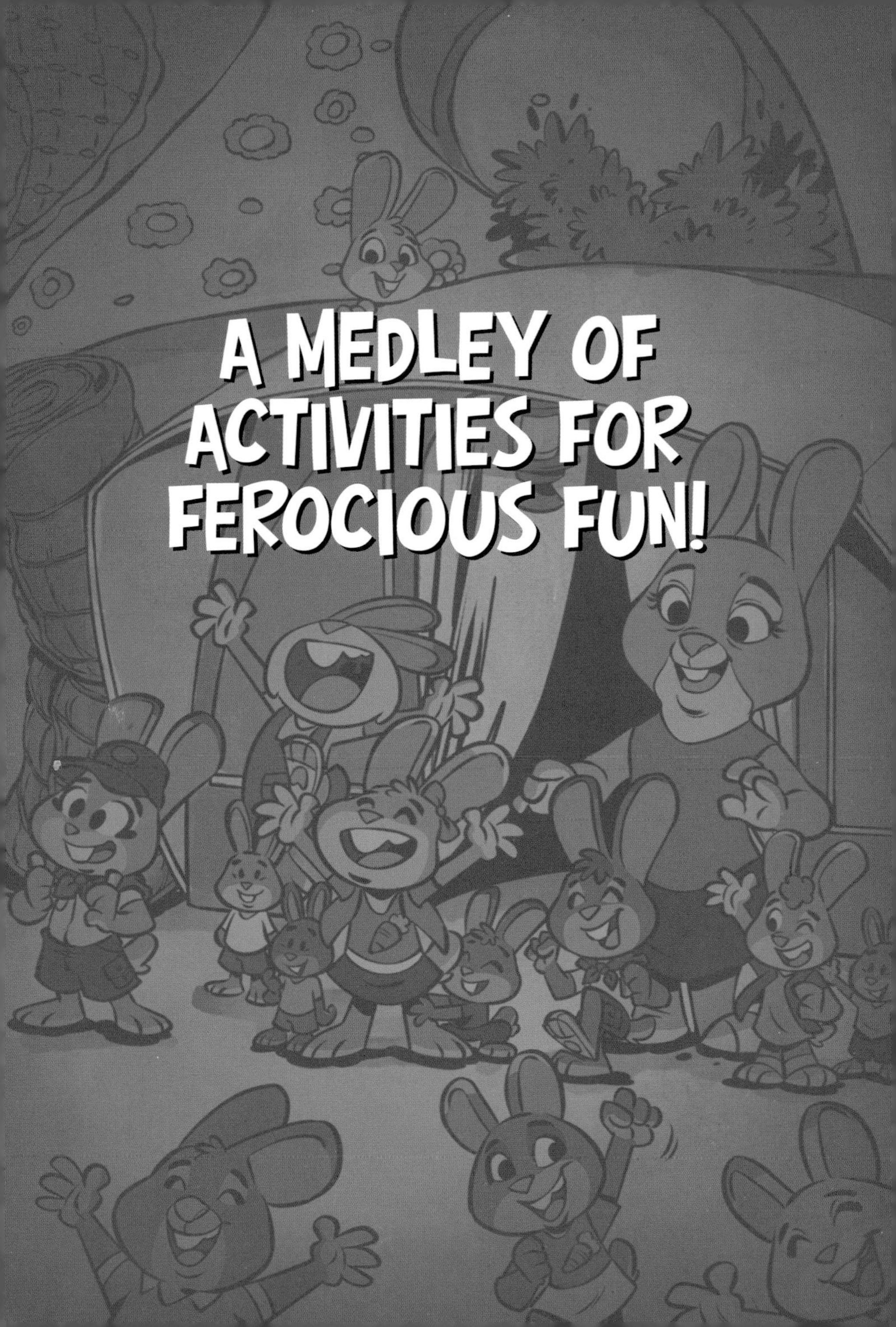

TELL ME A STORY. . .

ON HIS JOURNEY TO BUY THE PERFECT GIFT, NICK ENCOUNTERS MANY FRIENDS AND EXCHANGES MANY ITEMS WITH THEM. CAN YOU COME UP WITH A STORY ABOUT ONE OF THE OTHER CHARACTERS NICK MEETS DURING THE "TICKET CHASE" STORY? WHAT ADVENTURES DID THEIR NEWLY ACQUIRED ITEMS TAKE THEM ON?

WHERE DID THE TIGER GO WITH HIS NEW ROLLER SKATES?

WHAT DID THE BEAVER DO WITH THE BUNNY PUPPET?

CHOOSE ONE OF THE CHARACTER PATHS AND THINK ABOUT WHAT HAPPENED AFTER WE STOPPED FOLLOWING THEIR STORY. WRITE A STORY OR DRAW A PICTURE OF WHAT HAPPENS NEXT!

WHAT DID THE RACCOON BUY WITH THE EXTRA CASH HE RECEIVED?

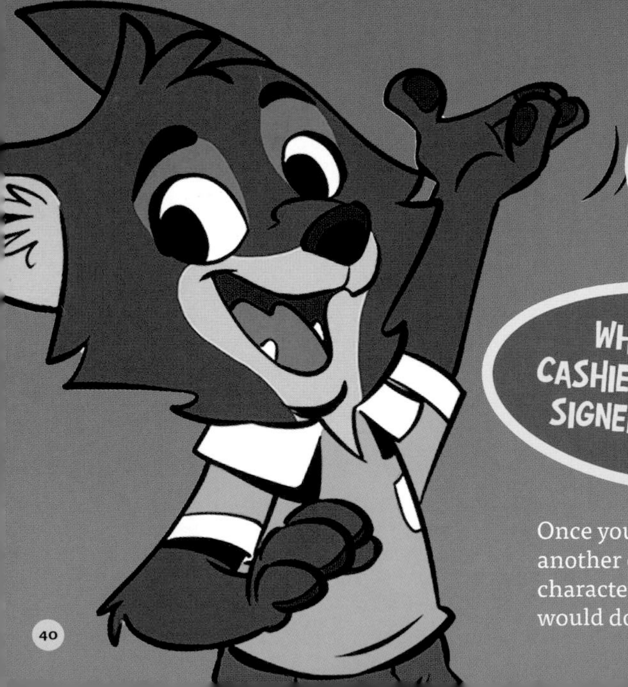

WHAT TRICKS WAS THE BEAR ABLE TO DO ON HIS NEW BIKE?

WHAT DID THE CASHIER DO WITH HIS SIGNED BASEBALL?

Once you've created one story, make another one! Try choosing a different character, or think about what *you* would do in those situations!

SCAVENGER HUNT!

CAN YOU FIND THESE ITEMS IN THE "TICKET CHASE" STORY?

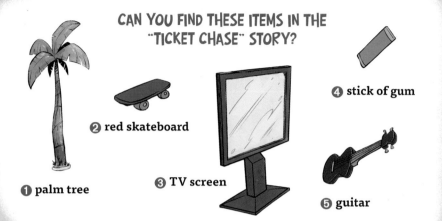

❶ palm tree

❷ red skateboard

❸ TV screen

❹ stick of gum

❺ guitar

CAN YOU FIND THESE ITEMS IN "THE GREAT INDOORS" STORY?

❶ carrot pen

❷ red book

❸ vase of flowers

❹ toaster

❺ lantern

Scavenger Hunt answer key:
"Ticket Chase": palm tree, page 17; red skateboard, page 14; TV screen, page 17; stick of gum, page 8; guitar, page 20

Scavenger Hunt answer key:
"The Great Indoors": carrot pen, page 25; red book, page 27; vase of flowers, page 30; toaster, page 33; lantern, page 25

WHAT'S MISSING FROM THE PICTURE?

LOOK AT THE TWO PICTURES ON THESE PAGES OF JUDY AND HER DAD GOING SHOPPING FOR THEIR CAMPING TRIP. IT'S THE SAME PICTURE . . . OR IS IT? CAN YOU SPOT 10 DIFFERENCES BETWEEN PICTURE A, AND PICTURE B? THERE ARE SOME THINGS MISSING!

WHEN YOU THINK YOU'VE FOUND ALL THE DIFFERENCES YOU CAN CHECK YOUR ANSWERS AT THE BOTTOM OF PAGE 44!

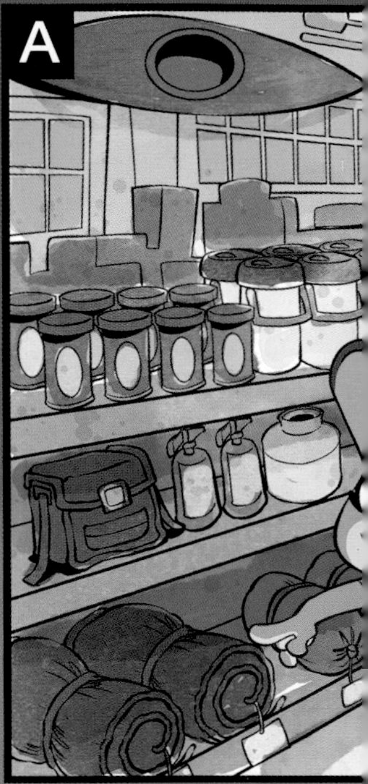
A

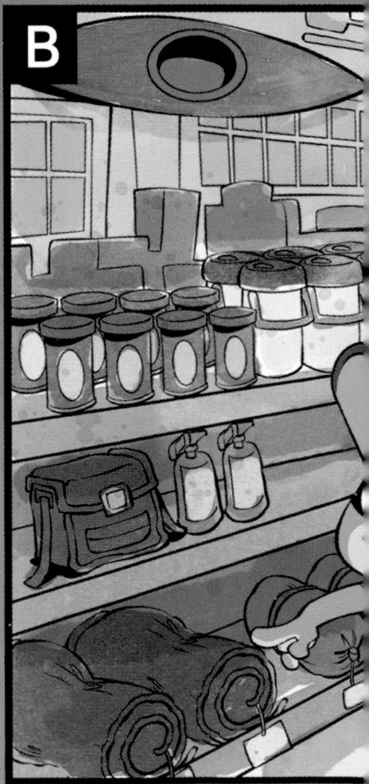
B

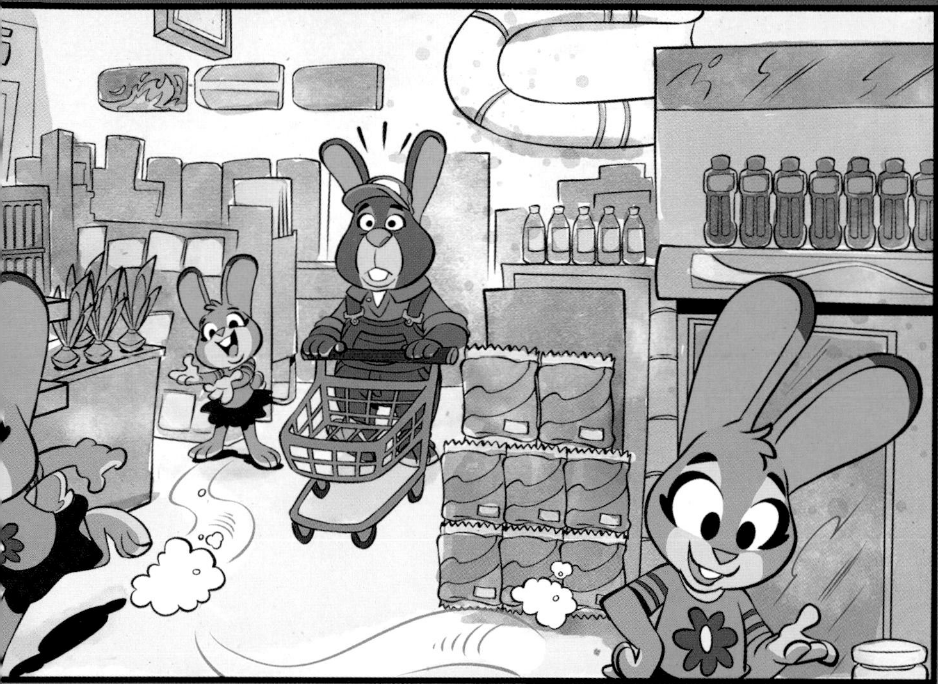

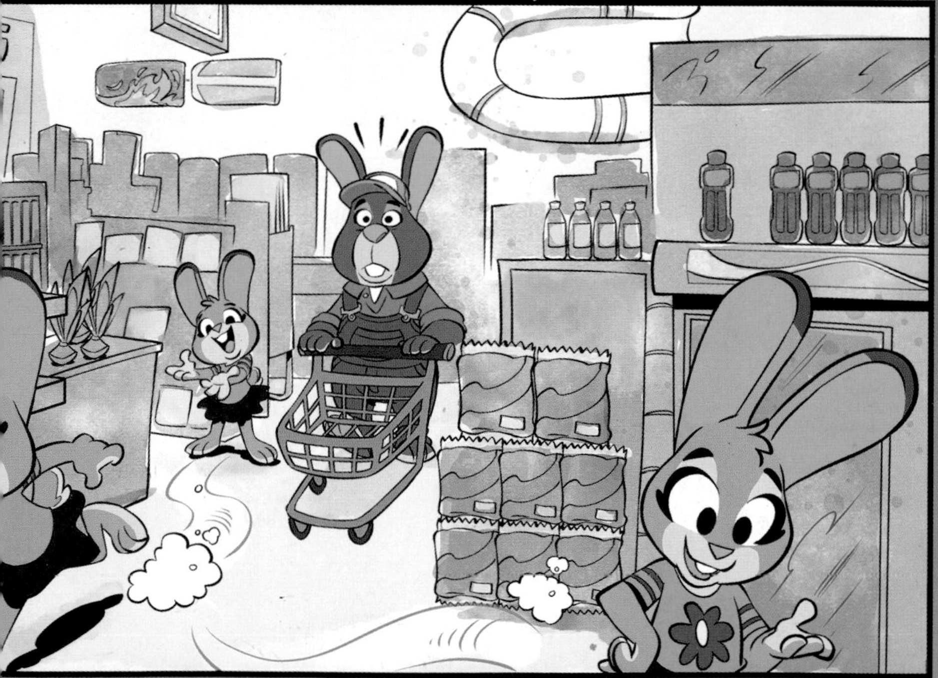

WHAT IS AN ALLITERATION?

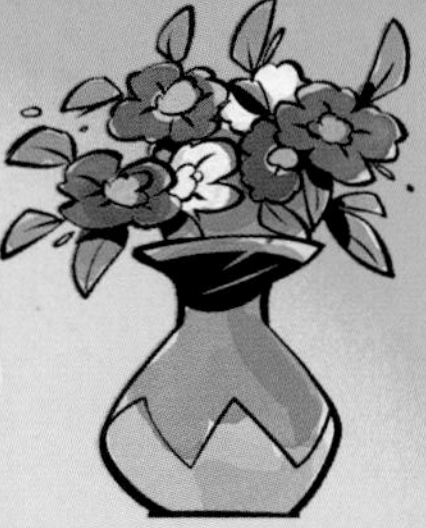

AN ALLITERATION IS THE REPETITION OF THE SAME SOUND IN A SERIES OF CONNECTED WORDS. THE REPEATED SOUND IS OFTEN AT THE BEGINNING OF THE WORDS IN THE SERIES, WHICH MEANS THAT WORDS IN AN ALLITERATION OFTEN BEGIN WITH THE SAME LETTER. BUT THE REPEATED SOUND CAN HAPPEN IN THE MIDDLE OR END OF THE WORDS IN AN ALLITERATION, TOO!

In "The Great Indoors," Judy's dad reads off a list of animal repellents that are examples of simple alliterations:

Bear Begone
Bear Busting
Fox Flustering
Barely There Bear

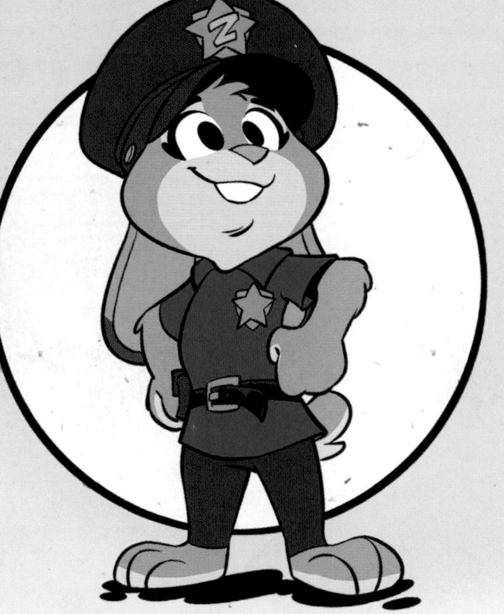

Can you think of some alliterations for Judy? You can use alliteration to describe her or make a sentence! To start, think about things you know about Judy, and try thinking of any words, adjectives, verbs, or nouns that start with the letter or sound of a "J." Here are a few of sentences that use alliteration . . .

Judy Jumps Joyfully.
Judy is on a Jaunt for Justice.
Judy is Just.

Alliterations are a fun way to get you thinking about sounds and rhythm! After you try making some alliterations for Judy, try it with other characters, or perhaps with an activity like camping!

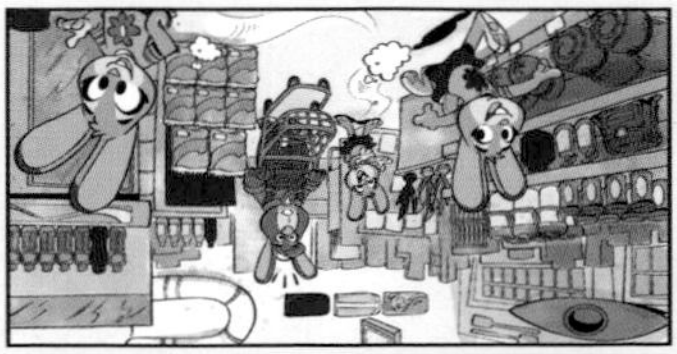

What's Missing from the Picture answer key:

STORY RECALL!

JUDY AND HER DAD'S CAMPING TRIP DIDN'T GO QUITE AS PLANNED, BUT THEY STILL HAD A LOT OF FUN! DO YOU REMEMBER THE DETAILS OF THEIR STORY? TRY YOUR BEST TO ANSWER THE QUESTIONS BELOW FROM MEMORY. IF YOU CAN'T REMEMBER THE ANSWERS TO THEM ALL, CHALLENGE YOURSELF TO READ THE STORY AGAIN AND FIND THE ANSWERS!

1. What was the first item Judy suggested buying at the store?
2. What two animals did Judy's dad want to buy repellent for?
3. What do the kids eat while listening to Judy's dad's scary story?
4. What kind of nose cream does Judy's dad want to buy?
5. What item does Judy give to her dad at the end of the story?
6. What does Judy's dad sleep in while "lamping" (living room camping)?
7. What day are Judy and her dad celebrating by going camping?
8. What Bunny Scouts badge will Judy earn for going camping?
9. What tool does Judy's dad use to fix the roof?
10. What does Judy use to catch the rain drops leaking?

Story Recall! answer key:
1) A tent; 2) Bears and Foxes; 3) Marshmallows; 4) Barely There Bear repellent nose cream; 5) Bear Be Gone spray; 6) A Sleeping bag; 7) Daddy-Daughter Day; 8) Outdoorsmanship badge; 9) A Hammer; 10) Pots and pans.

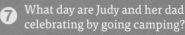

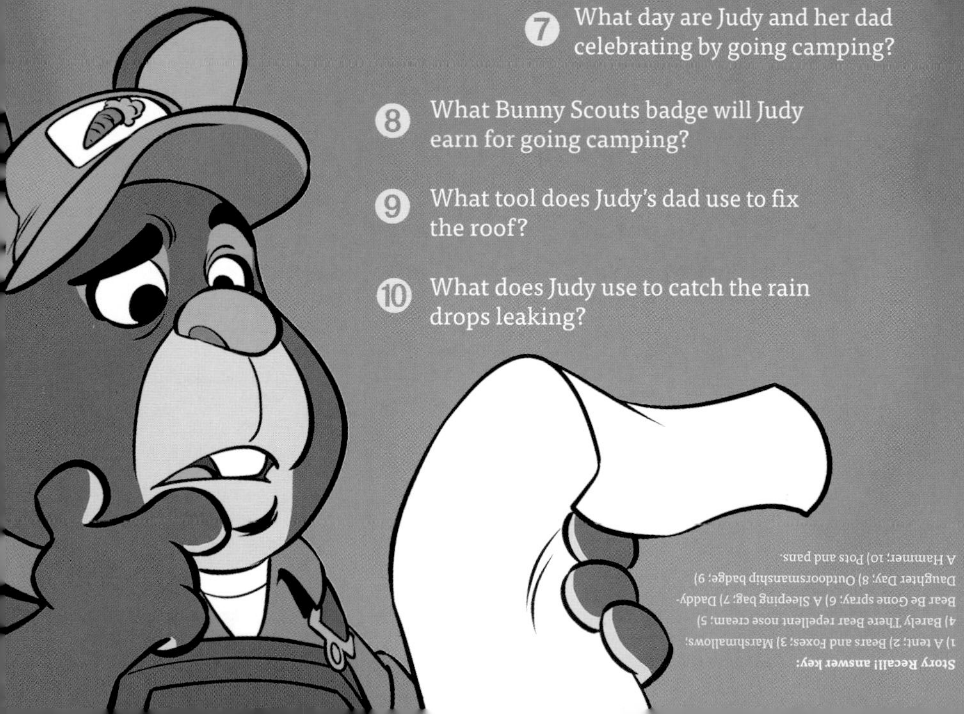

MAKE AN ACROSTIC POEM!

WHAT EXACTLY IS AN ACROSTIC POEM? THIS TYPE OF POEM USES EACH OF THE LETTERS IN A TOPIC WORD TO BEGIN EACH LINE OF A POEM. THE LINES OF THIS POEM CAN BE SENTENCES, OR PHRASES, OR SINGLE WORDS—BUT EACH LINE MUST DESCRIBE OR RELATE TO THE TOPIC WORD.

Now that you know a little about acrostic poems, let's create some! You can try it here (or on a separate piece of paper) using the names of the characters from the story as topic words!

Using each letter in Nick's first and last name, think of one word that starts with that letter that could describe him.

N. ....

I. ....

C. ....

K. ....

W. ....

I. ....

L. ....

D. ....

E. ....

Turning Nick's name into an acrostic poem give it a lot more meaning! What other names could you try this game with . . . Perhaps try it with your *own name*?

DARK HORSE BOOKS

president and publisher Mike Richardson • collection editor Freddye Miller •
collection assistant editor Judy Khuu • collection designer David Nestelle
• digital art technician Christianne Gillenardo-Goudreau

Neil Hankerson Executive Vice President • Tom Weddle Chief Financial Officer • Randy Stradley Vice President of
Publishing • Nick McWhorter Chief Business Development Officer • Matt Parkinson Vice President of Marketing • Dale
LaFountain Vice President of Information Technology • Cara Niece Vice President of Production and Scheduling • Mark
Bernardi Vice President of Book Trade and Digital Sales • Ken Lizzi General Counsel • Dave Marshall Editor in Chief •
Davey Estrada Editorial Director • Chris Warner Senior Books Editor • Cary Grazzini Director of Specialty Projects • Lia
Ribacchi Art Director • Vanessa Todd-Holmes Director of Print Purchasing • Matt Dryer Director of Digital Art
and Prepress • Michael Gombos Director of International Publishing and Licensing •
Kari Yadro Director of Custom Programs

DISNEY PUBLISHING WORLDWIDE GLOBAL MAGAZINES, COMICS AND PARTWORKS

PUBLISHER Lynn Waggoner • EDITORIAL TEAM Bianca Coletti (Director, Magazines), Guido Frazzini (Director, Comics),
Carlotta Quattrocolo (Executive Editor), Stefano Ambrosio (Executive Editor, New IP), Camilla Vedove (Senior Manager,
Editorial Development), Behnoosh Khalili (Senior Editor), Julie Dorris (Senior Editor), Mina Riazi (Assistant Editor),
Jonathan Manning (Assistant Editor) • DESIGN Enrico Soave (Senior Designer) • ART Ken Shue (VP, Global Art), Manny
Mederos (Senior Illustration Manager, Comics and Magazines), Roberto Santillo (Creative Director), Marco Ghiglione
(Creative Manager), Stefano Attardi (Computer Art Designer) • PORTFOLIO MANAGEMENT Olivia Ciancarelli (Director)
• BUSINESS & MARKETING Mariantonietta Galla (Marketing Manager), Virpi Korhonen (Editorial Manager))

Zootopia: Family Night

Published by Dark Horse Books
A division of Dark Horse Comics LLC.
10956 SE Main Street
Milwaukie, OR 97222

DarkHorse.com

To find a comics shop in your area, visit comicshoplocator.com

First edition: March 2019
ISBN 978-1-50671-053-2
Digital ISBN 978-1-50671-060-0

1 3 5 7 9 10 8 6 4 2
Printed in China

LOOKING FOR BOOKS FOR YOUNGER READERS?

DISNEY·PIXAR INCREDIBLES 2: HEROES AT HOME

While their mom and dad—Mr. Incredible and Elastigirl—are both taking on new and very different jobs, Dash and Violet are doing their best to help out! First, Dash and Violet go into secret Super mode when they interrupt criminal activity on a routine grocery trip to pick up some essentials! Then, helping out at home, their efforts to keep up on their chores are unknowingly obstructed by the innocent mischief of their little brother, Jack-Jack!

ISBN 978-1-50670-943-7 | $7.99

DISNEY ZOOTOPIA: FRIENDS TO THE RESCUE

Young Judy Hopps is excited for the fun at the Bunnyburrow County Fair, but her friend Dinah has to sneak out of the house to join her! When Dinah stumbles into trouble, it takes both Judy and Dinah's talents to ensure that they both make it safely home. Meanwhile, at his friend Hedy's birthday party, young Nick Wilde learns it's the thought that counts. While he might not have enough money to buy a gift, Nick has other talents that he puts to good use for a truly unforgettable celebration.

ISBN 978-1-50671-054-9 | $7.99